Eleven Plus by Martin Wilkes

Chapter 1: Eleven Plus

Music has a unique way of triggering nostalgic memories. My clock-radio roused me from my slumbers, with a blast-from-the-past called Excerpt from a Teenage Opera. This song instantly transported my brain back, half-a-century, to my eleventh year of life.

"Count the days, into years......," sang Keith West, opening synaptic connections to a memory of a memory.

It was a summer's day in 1966 and my mind was back in my old bed, in our council house in Sutton Green. This council estate, in the centre of England, was the epicentre of my life. It was a momentous day - being the first day of hols since leaving Junior school. There was another important matter but my hypnagogic state was clouding my thoughts. Forgetfulness was my Achilles heel, my specific weakness, according to my brother, Andrew. He happened to be the cleverest 13-year-old that I knew and he did not have an Achilles heel.

I checked the clock. It was 7:15 a.m.

"Grocer Jack, Grocer Jack, get off your back……..," Keith West's song blared out. My sympathies lay with Grocer Jack because I was truly enjoying the pleasures of staying in bed. Mum had started her wash day routine particularly early, making sure we all shared the Tony Blackburn Show on Radio One. It was her way of establishing with dad that the six-week holiday was 'no holiday for mothers!'

As I considered the reality of my looming transition to high school, I thought to myself, *"Good riddance to Marston Road Junior and Infants School,"* The first day of the summer hols traditionally meant that mum would be presenting a minefield of moods. However, in the short term, it was blissful to just lay there while my brain savoured a montage of memories, spanning from 1959 to 1966.

I pondered my days in the nursery school, as a 4-year-old, where Mrs Flood lined everyone up in front of a giant jar of cod liver oil. She used the same spoon to slap a dollop of the greyish brown goo onto each child's tongue, probably spreading as many diseases as she was trying to prevent. I had haunting recollections of Yellow Fish Fridays, when they fed us disgusting Finney Haddock - even if it made us vomit; even if we had already vomited on Boiled Liver Thursday! Nursery had no room for finicky eaters.

The bedrooms in our Sutton Green home were always cold, despite the estate being the flagship of Staffordshire's council. In 1964, we had moved a few houses up the road, from a two-bedroom house, to a three-bedroom corner plot. Unfortunately, the bend was more exposed and the bedrooms were particularly plagued with cold. The ambient temperature simply made the bed more difficult to vacate, so I wallowed in nostalgia under the warmth of my blankets, ignoring the nagging feeling of procrastination. I had had that sensation most of my life, so I wasn't unduly perturbed. Doodle, the family cat added to my contentment, as he lay under the covers with me, with his motor running full throttle.

Mum poignantly cranked up the radio, as Keith West proclaimed, "Husbands moan at breakfast tables, no milk, no eggs, no marmalade labels."

Meanwhile, I reminisced about post-lunch nursery nap times. Mrs Timpson, the most dominant of the three teachers, had always insisted that everyone lay silent on canvas beds for the longest half-hour of the day.

"It's a smack-bottom for anybody who isn't asleep by the time I count to ten," she would announce. For those of us who had grasped numeracy, it was irresistible to not count along.

"At least we were learning about counting," my semi-awake brain reflected; by eleven I was starting to experiment with sarcasm. Andrew saw this as the highest form of humour and he actively encouraged it.

One day, Mrs Timpson demanded, "Who's trumped?" as we lay fake-sleeping. There was a particularly acrid stench in the room, one of those pungencies that eats into your gums. When nobody confessed, Mrs Timpson directed Miss Flood and Mrs Rhodes to sniff everyone's bottom, until they homed in on the culprit. A smack-bottom was duly awarded to Johnny Marston, which would have been fair, except that Johnny had Down's Syndrome.

"The nursery showed no favours to farting Mongols," my cynical-self mused, in a time before the term was offensive. I was suddenly extra glad that I would never again set foot in an environment where mandatory buttock-sniffing was acceptable.

I adjusted my pillow, as I recalled how proud I had been to move into the real school - no naptime there! Miss Ellis's class was where I learned how to tie shoelaces, and read Janet and John books, which focused entirely upon upper class children. They flew kites, played on the swing, rode bikes, took picnics, walked the dog, and their mother was always baking cakes.

Miss Ellis was a kind-hearted spinster, who saw all of us as her personal children. I wondered how she ever survived six-weeks holiday because her class was her entire life. Even when she was being strict, we knew that it was 'for our own good' and she never smacked Johnny Marston, whatever his state of flatulence.

Next, I progressed to Mrs Forsythe's class. Her moods ranged from entrancing to borderline psychotic. She made the perverse choice of delegating me the role of ink monitor, which brought daily chastisements. Spillages at school regularly earned me a publicly humiliating plimsoll to the bottom; and ink damage to my clothes brought me further admonishment when I got home. I never discovered that Mrs Forsythe did not hate me until I'd moved into the more progressive Mr Lockett's class. His relaxed style suited me but he was considered a bit of a softy by the rest of the school staff. Of all my teachers, Mr Lockett was the only one who did not put us through laborious hands-on-heads, fingers-on-lips routines just to demonstrate who was in control. It was Lockett who first discovered and nurtured my lightning speed, culminating in me winning the City Sports sixty-yard dash and having my picture on the front page of the Evening Sentinel back in 1965.

I was almost enjoying school until the next move, to Mrs Heath's class. She could never understand that football was my entire life, and yet she exploited my obsession, by always threatening to hold me back from the school team. Her strict approach probably forced me to learn more than Mr. Lockett but it was a miserable year. Mrs Heath was like an angry Mrs Forsythe and she prided herself on setting the highest of standards. In reality, it meant that every student left her class with lower self-esteem than when they entered.

I recalled how Mrs Heath had made me the Toilet Monitor, giving me the job of making sure that everyone resisted peeing contests, flushed the chains, and washed their hands before lunch. I recalled how Gary Roberts had decided that I was taking my job too seriously and punched me on the nose. As my nose cracked, I simultaneously banged the back of my head against the wall and learned what "seeing stars" actually meant. I am not sure how long I was 'out cold' but when I came around Mrs Heath was standing over me, oblivious to my bloodied nose, ordering me to check that all three toilets had been flushed, and not to forget to wash my own hands. I had felt lousy all afternoon, and then the 3-mile walk home had felt exhausting. I had blood on my t-shirt and was a bit concerned that my mum would be mad. But it was not like the old days, because, even though my awkward streak irritated her, she had gotten better at controlling her temper with me. When I was eight-years-old things came to a head when I accused her of bullying me and she had a moment of lucidity, when she realized that she was merely recycling the abuse that her wicked mother had inflicted on her.

In reality, I flopped down in the chair and mum instantly said, "Oh my God, who broke your nose?"

Mum was mad but it was at Mrs Heath, for her apparent callousness. Dad was mad, too, and he put me in the car and drove me straight around to Gary Roberts house.

"Look what your son has done to my boy's nose," he yelled at the huge father of Gary Roberts.

"I can't see anything!" Gary's father, who happened to be a policeman, responded. He obviously knew the law.

"He's put three knuckle marks in my son's nose," dad continued unperturbed.

"Gary, come here!" he insisted. Gary sheepishly walked to the doorway. I felt sorry for him, in that moment. "Gary, did you do this?"

"No dad," replied the boy. My sympathy instantly disappeared.

"That's the end of that then," insisted the policeman. Dad and I both knew that he was right.

The knock-on effect of having a broken nose was that I had to have an operation to fix it, while the rest of my school-friends went off to the Isle of Man, on a joint school trip between Marston Road and Cranston Road schools. All my friends came back with tales of adventure and romance. Sally Doyle, my love interest, who had been flirting with me for three years, starting with love letters and developing into several pecks on the cheek, had apparently snogged 'Funny Michael Johnson.' I just knew that her lips were intended for mine and I was a little put out that I was so easily substituted. I was not sure whether Funny Mike was just any-port-in-a-storm or whether she lost interest in me when I let Gary Roberts break my nose. Either way, I was a tad hurt. That trip sounded tremendous and mum vowed that she'd make sure that I got to go the following year.

Tony Blackburn interjected, with a smooth and hilarious segue, "Well it doesn't sound like Grocer Jack's doing the rounds today. Maybe the Mama's and Papa's can remind him what day it is?"

"Monday, Monday," started Mama Cass, right on cue.

Still snuggled down in bed, I remembered the relief of moving into Mr Barton's class. He understood football tactics and I knew that he would never blackmail me with team selections, the way that Heath had. Then I remember resenting it when Mr Barton was replaced by Mr Tattersfield half-way through the year.

Irrelevant of my blankets, I had a warm feeling of pride as I remembered that I had recently passed my 11-plus exam, meaning that I would be spending the next seven years at the best boys' school in Staffordshire: Hartley High School. Only Anton Zelesky and Barry Cooper had managed to match this achievement: Zellie had always been a shoe-in; I was considered highly probable; but Cooper's enrolment into the all-boys grammar school was no less than a minor miracle.

Cooper was a genius with a football; he was six inches smaller than me, but really strong. Whilst I had long legs and phenomenal acceleration, Cooper had a low centre of gravity and he could turn on a sixpence to shield the ball. He was great to have on your side but no fun to play against because he could easily 'make a monkey of you.' Often, defenders became impatient and tried to hack his legs from under him. Then it was like watching a matador teasing a big clumsy bull. He was pretty good at art and he had a wicked sense of humour but his academic skills were not at all apparent. One bonus was that he had an 'in' with all the Staffordshire schoolboys, who had coincidentally also managed to pass their 11-pluses. The likes of Robert Bobbington and Lee Anderson, already legends, would be gracing the same football fields as myself. They had already had scouts from Port Vale watching them. A world with football scouts sounded sublime; maybe they would spot my Billy-the-Whizz wing play.

"It never hurts to try," my dad always told me. He had started to show me a little more respect, or maybe a little less contempt, since my unpredicted city sports victory. It would have been his ultimate dream for me to be a footballer. Now he heard that I was going to be hobnobbing with the city's creme de la creme.

"I'm not playing for the Vale!" I protested. Dad was mainly a Stoke fan but he had grown up in Smallthorne, half-a-mile away from Vale Park and he had an affection for them, too. There's no way I'd ever play for the Vale. I was a Stoke City man, through and through.

Needless-to-say, my elder brother, Andrew had already been at Hartley High for two years. He was the family brain box. I was always respected for my speed and agility, rather than my academics. Having been eternally eclipsed by my brother's phenomenal memory and concentration skills it felt truly splendid to achieve something in my own right - probable or not!

As I lay in bed, my mind meandering between dreams and wakefulness, I savoured my success. Mum and dad were beginning to recognize my maturation. They were starting to refer to me as a possible 'late bloomer,' as opposed to 'scatterbrain' or 'bloody idiot!'

I had reached a natural crossroads – a perfect time for an image overhaul. No longer would I have to plan my life around avoiding Ivy Morrison and Sandra Adams - two girls hell-bent on making me blush. There would be no girls at Hartley High School. Anyway, Ivy would be going to Horton Lane Secondary Modern, where she would receive a less 'classical' education. She would be learning about sewing, typing and cookery, whilst the boys at Hartley High were studying trigonometry, French and physics. Still, at least she would have members of the opposite sex to embarrass mercilessly.

Maybe I could finally shake off the endless worrying about trivia - forgotten dinner money; misplaced football boots; unrehearsed spelling tests – you name it, I worried. Never a day went by at Marston Road Junior School when there was not something plaguing my inner peace. Yet, I had survived and emerged triumphant. The self-denigration and nagging doubts would hold no place in my new image. I would vow this to myself, as I lay in my bed, listening to Tony Blackburn. He was my favourite DJ, a remnant from pirate radio. He had the confidence I could only dream of and he used to chunter witticisms to himself between hit songs.

"So, here's a song by Chris Farlowe called "Out of Time" he said adding, "which is crazy. You should have asked me Chris and I would have told you it's 7:30, on this beautiful Monday morning."

The music started, "Baby, baby, baby, you're out of time," sang Chris Farlowe, unaware that, like Keith West, he would also soon be obsolete. My clock clicked to Seven thirty a.m., confirming Tony Blackburn's time check.

Chapter 2: The Manx Maid

"Seven thirty? Seven thirty! Dad!" I screamed. I suddenly remembered what I was supposed to be doing. Remarkably, the whole family had forgotten, too. I was due to be setting off to the Isle of Man, on my year-late make-up holiday. Mum had had me packing for days. How could she suddenly forget?

"Bloody Hell!" my dad replied from their bedroom.

I was supposed to be at Etruria Station at 7:55 a.m. This was at least thirty minutes away.

"Baby, baby, baby you're out of time." Chris Farlowe insisted on reminding me.

I ripped off my pyjamas and threw them into the bulging suitcase. Andrew helped, by sitting on it, whilst I aligned the latches. In ten seconds, I was fully dressed. With no wash, no breakfast and no hope, mum whisked me into the front seat of our Sunbeam Rapier. Dad did not even allow himself the luxury of clothes. Instead, he donned his ugly checked dressing gown over his hideous striped pyjamas.

"We'll never make it!" I protested.

"I've paid ten quid, for this bloody holiday!" dad countered, "maybe the train will be late?"

"Dad it's not a bloody PMT bus, it's a train!" I cursed. Even in this anxious state, when I heard my own voice swearing at dad, I flinched, half expecting a reprisal. I was a high school student, now. Dad gave me an empathetic glance. He'd been showing me more respect ever since I'd passed my Eleven Plus.

"Good luck," yelled mum as we raced done Bladon Circle, past our previous abode and to the corner. The tyres screeched, as we took the bend at about fifty miles per hour. Dad was usually a cautious driver but with the double motivation of not losing ten quid and, also getting me out of the house for a week, we broke all records on the Sutton Green to Etruria Grand Prix!

He switched on the car radio hoping for a time check. The signal drifted in and out, as The

Spencer Davis Band urged us to, "Keep on Running!" I felt like Tony Blackburn was straight forward 'taking the piss,' by this point. He seemed to be providing the soundtrack of my life. Since then, I have discovered that most songs have relevance to most aspects of life. Just like the eyes on a painting seem to follow you around the room, music can punctuate your life, whenever you are receptive to it.

Amazingly, the train was still in the station when we arrived and, with his dressing gown gaping, belt dragging and pyjama cord hanging, dad grabbed me and my suitcase and ran full pelt down the steps to the platform, with me fireman's-lifted over his shoulders. Knowing the nature of those kind of pyjamas, I was now praying that 'Little Pete' did not decide to put in an appearance, as we bounced toward the train. Luckily, things held together on that front.

I could see that the train guard was about to whistle off the train, when the spectacle of our arrival forced him to pause. It was probably against protocol, but playing it to the letter would have resulted in him being left alone with a crying teenager and an angry parent - who was dressed like he might have escaped from an insane asylum. Furthermore, Mr Tattersfield's wife, who was a teacher at Cranston Road School, saw the situation developing and insisted that Mr Tattersfield open the train door to prevent departure, albeit at considerable risk to himself. Against all odds, I made the train.

And, so it was that I started my long trip to the Isle of Man: flustered and humiliated. It was an altogether weird situation because my parents had insisted on honouring their pledge to send me on the trip that all my friends had experienced twelve months prior. However, having enjoyed the perfect holiday the year before, nobody from Marston Road wanted to improve on perfection, or at least their parents did not want to pay for it a second time. This had somehow developed a reputation, amongst the Cranston Road ruffians, that Marston Roaders were standoffish, if not outright snobs. It was under this guise that I first encountered them.

"This is Martin Wells, he's from Marston Road. Make room for him!" announced Mr. Hansen, as he bundled me into a full carriage. Theoretically, there was room for eight kids in a carriage, and since there were only six, there should have been space. Unfortunately, they were already spread out, three girls on one side, each needing additional space for their handbags. To make things worse, I realized that two of the boys and one of the girls were members of the legendary Trotter family. They had a reputation of being 'scary bad' and they had an elder brother, Sean, who was the terror of Hanley and the shot-caller at the local borstal.

After deliberately ignoring me, purely to enjoy my embarrassment, it was Kenny, the older

Trotter, who cleared space next to him and gestured that I sit there. Legend has it that Kenny had indulged in some seriously heavy petting with Ivy Morrison, my arch-nemesis, the previous year so that was another reason to be cautious.

"Feel this!" he told me, indicating a protrusion stemming from his trousers and extending up under his shirt.

"I'm okay, thanks," I responded, as politely as I could. But his insistent glare, along with a gasp from his peers, told me that this was not the end of the interaction.

"Feel it!" he reiterated. So, I grabbed hold of the rock-hard protrusion, and squeezed, trying to be as nonchalant as possible, under the circumstances.

"What is it?" I asked.

"My dick," he snickered, the rest of the compartment laughed.

"No?" I responded, as ambiguously as I could, at the same time as trying to fight my repulsion. I wasn't sure if I was allowed to let go or not so I just held on for grim life until he indicated otherwise.

"Nair, it's a knife," he eventually revealed. Sure enough, he lifted his shirt to show that I had my hands on the shaft of a flick-knife. Now, I was relieved that it wasn't the shaft of his dick but shocked about the knife. Possession of such a weapon would definitely put him in the same borstal as his brother, Shaun.

"Can I let go now," I asked, pulling my hand away.

John Trotter, Ken's younger brother, thought that this was hilarious for some reason, and his laughter broke the tension in the room.

"He's funny, Ken," laughed John, "This kid's funny!"

Kenny chuckled, too. From that moment, Kenny accepted me, which meant that his friends respected me. Barry Wise, the non-Trotter, offered me a piece of his Kit-Kat chocolate bar. I was conflicted between the social etiquette and the pangs of hunger resulting from a skipped breakfast. Furthermore, I had a determination to alter my image as I moved into the next phase of life. The old me would have humbly declined but the new, friend-of-the-Trotter's-me politely accepted and gobbled it down. Kenny laughed again. Barry frowned, not so much that I had taken his food, it was more that he was seeing his role of jester being threatened. John Trotter was also an amusing person but, unlike Barry, he had a style of making people laugh 'with' him, rather than 'at' him. I felt an empathy with John because he had developed humour as a survival tactic in the family-from-Hell. I could relate because I often used jocularity to diffuse conflict in my own dysfunctional family. John timed his delivery with an enviable expertise. He, sort of had you sitting on the edge of your seat awaiting his humorous retorts. Sometimes what he said was not particularly funny but everyone was pre-conditioned to laugh. This was someone from whom I could learn, as I endeavoured to rebuild my image for high school.

The girls in the carriage were interesting. Sammy Jeffries was obviously interested in Kenny. She was one of those girls who had a fully developed bosom at the age of eleven. She had an exaggerated infectious laugh, making her the perfect audience for the carriage of jokesters. Apparently, there had been a cat-fight between Sammy and Ivy Morrison the previous year. I had to believe that Ivy would not have stood a chance. Sammy's side-kick, Andrea was the same age but a foot smaller and she looked young for her age. Andrea tended to echo every gesture that Sammy made.

By the time, we were changing trains at Crewe Station, the Trotter entourage insisted that I stay with them for the stretch to Liverpool. The quiet, young sister spent most of the journey holding a transistor radio tight against her left ear. Every so often, the tuning tended to go in and out as the train navigated bends and tunnels but one of her brothers would say, "Oh I like this one, turn it up," and we would be subject to whistling, crackling bastardizations of our 'fave raves.'

A new song by The Kinks, called Dedicated Follower of Fashion was introduced and John Trotter immediately said, "Oh I like this one, turn it up Sonja."

Sonja obliged, adding, "You only like it because you are one!" It was true, John Trotter's maroon hipsters and turquoise long sleeved nylon shirt cast him as a fashion guru. He prided himself on his mod clothes and the whole carriage was comfortable to laugh at this joke, which had obviously earned previous success. She looked over to me for approval. I exaggerated my laugh to accentuate that I was part of the team. Sonja was clearly twelve months younger than me. Barry Wise was obviously a little smitten with her but everyone could see that his devotions were unrequited.

John Trotter shared his Cheese and Branston Pickle sandwich with me, as we pulled into Lime Street station in Liverpool. An hour later, John Trotter and I both re-shared his Cheese and Branston Pickle sandwiches with the fishes of the Irish Sea, as everyone hung over the deck of the Manx Maid. We had started by adopting an out-of-sight-out-of-mind approach to the sea's fierce rolling, pitching and yawing, by going into the ship's lower cabins. Once a couple of weak-stomached students had filled the room with puke fumes, empathetic reverse peristalsis kicked in and it was like a race to the decks. The Irish Sea had decided to take this day to show us that it's power was a great leveller. Catfight queen, Sammy Jeffries emptied her stomach contents over the side, hipster John Trotter wretched, knife-yielding Kenny Trotter projectile vomited, hugely overweight Mrs.Tattersfield discovered bulimia. Headmaster,

Mr. Hansen felt a need to demonstrate leadership by resisting his revulsions. But eventually, he humiliated himself as a powerful gust of wind intercepted his sea-bound upchuck, held it almost suspended in mid-air and then splattered him full in the face.

"Return to Sender!" sang John Trotter, quoting an old Elvis Presley song. It was literally one of those jokes that was not funny at the time, but became more and more hilarious with retellings.

The boat's tannoy chose to try and distract us by blasting out the latest pop songs. Unfortunately, The Beach Boys, Sloop John B seemed a little too appropriate. As Brian Wilson sang, "I wanna go home," we were equally disenchanted with the Manx Maid.

The irony of this nightmare shared experience was that it seemed to form a common camaraderie, in the face of adversity. We all stayed on deck for the rest of the journey and started to gain our sea legs. The Irish Sea had shown everyone that nature has the upper hand and then started to show its other side. By the time, we pulled into Douglas harbour the sea hardly gave ripple. The amazing thing about sea sickness is that, you feel like you've got malaria as it happens but an hour later you can feel on top of the world again. By the time, we were loaded onto the rented coach to Douglas High School, where we were staying, everyone was in good spirits, singing the traditional

Cliff Richard Mantra, "We're all going on a Summer Holiday," and ready for fun.

It's hard to know what we were expecting, when we got to the dormitories. However, we all thought that our parents' ten pounds should have purchased a little more luxury than the two old classrooms, one for boys one for girls, with a sleeping bag and canvas bed each. It suddenly felt like nursery school again and we would be having our bottoms sniffed later.

After dinner, we took a brief walk around the grounds. Beautiful Rhododendron bushes brought colour to the campus, as well as providing numerous hiding places for a quick cigarette. It had seemed an age since I had been lying in my bed listening to Tony Blackburn, and I was glad when 'time for bed,' was declared.

Mr. Parker, the recently retired deputy headmaster from Cranston Road, was sent in to set expectations, while MrsTatts gave a similar speech to the girls. Parker was a guily, craggy-faced teacher who had learned to keep students on their toes by delivering serious and funny comments with a Poe face. He also knew how to effectively use pauses to maintain discipline.

"Firstly, it's lights out at ten o'clock," he stated, "Mr. Wise, what does lights out mean?"

"Switch the lights off, sir," replied Barry.

"Good, what else?" continued the teacher.

"No talking," Barry said.

"Exactly," Parker confirmed, "Who knows what jankers are?"

The group remained silent.

"Who would like to know what jankers are?" he asked.

After a pause, controlled purely by Mr. Parker's expression, Kenny Trotter raised his hand. This was followed by six more hands, including my own.

"Trust me, you don't want to know what jankers are," he insisted. Of course, now we all did want to know.

"Please sir, what are jankers?" John Trotter asked, to a titter which was instantly stifled by Parker's glare.

"Jankers are what they make the army do when they don't follow orders. Peeling potatoes, scrubbing toilets, mowing the lawn with a pair of scissors. Enough said?" he demanded. He had made his point.

"What time is it, Mr. Wise?" he asked.

"Ten o'clock, sir," said Barry.

Lights out. We all fell instantly asleep.

The next morning everyone was dressed in their most 'with it' clothes, ready to hit the town. Then Mr. Hansen decided to intervene. "It's going to be beautiful today, boys. You need to get some sun on those legs, so it's shorts day."

"Don't have any shorts, sir," declared Barry, thinking that would be the end of the matter.

"Nor me," insisted John Trotter.

"No problem, boys." he responded, emptying a kit bag of about 20 pairs of baggy faded blue football shorts onto the floor. Douglas High School won't mind us using their spares.

Personally, I was mortified at the thought of having to go out in public in these extremely uncool clothes. However, John Trotter went ashen in colour at the very idea.

"You can stick those up your, arse!" he said under his breath but not quite quietly enough.

"What did you say, Trotter?" asked the headmaster.

"I said 'what a farce,' sir." he retorted.

Mr. Hansen thought for a second and decided to accept the new version.

So, in what seemed like the cruellest thing that could happen, we made our first appearance on the town, dressed like we had just escaped from the orphanage. It seemed like it was going to be a week from hell but the next day we were allowed to wear our own clothes and we were happy to be alive again.

I bought some Consulate cigarettes, and suddenly I was as cool as the couple in the Consulate adverts.

"Crash the ash," Kenny Trotter told me, when he heard about my new acquisition. Sure enough, they were a cool smoke.

The culmination of the week came on the Wednesday, we heard that a group called, "The Move" was playing at the Pavilion Gardens. Sammy asked special permission for us to go and Mr. Hansen agreed that, "So long as you're in bed for lights out."

We were suddenly going to be watching a real, Top of the Pops group live. I was no longer a scallywag from Sutton Green; I was a jet-setter. We worked out that we could afford to get a taxi back from the concert, which would only take 12 minutes; we could probably leave the concert at 9:45 pm and still be back with three minutes to spare.

So, Barry, John, Andrea, Sammy and myself set off in our fanciest mod clothes. John Trotter lent me an ultra-mod cravat, to smarten up my shirt and jeans look, and we arrived at the Douglas Pavilion as the doors opened, feeling like the bee's knees.

Everyone in the place was so much older than us and I could see them nudging one another as we danced with the girls around their handbags. My four peers danced just like the Top of the Pops audience but I tended to just rock from one foot to the other. Andrea sensed my awkwardness and so grabbed my wrists and coaxed my movements into the rhythm. Like most things, it got worse before it got better. Then, I suddenly got it and this brought smile and nods of approval from the whole group. I can only liken it to the feeling you get when you learn to swim. Onlookers also smiled as we became quite the focal point in the room. It was already one of the best nights of my life. Then, The Move stole our attention. They had sneaked onstage whilst we were creating our diversion and as Roy Wood strummed the first chord of "Flowers in the Rain" a flurry of newspaper reporters appeared and photographers scampered toward the stage. There was controversy because, according to the New Musical Express, the band had smashed a statue of the English Prime Minister, Harold Wilson, during their act just the week before.

Unfortunately, at the end of the first song Barry pointed to his watch. It was already 10 O'clock. I was mortified because missing 'lights out' would mean teacher's wrath and the dreaded jankers!

"We have to go, I told the others, and we were halfway to the door, when the Move started singing John Trotter's favourite song, called Fire Brigade, and my gang all turned and ran back to watch more of the show.

"Cast your mind back ten years to the girl that's next to me at school," sang Roy Wood. "If I put my hand upon her leg she'd hit me with a rule."

It suddenly occurred to me that what we were doing could get us caned. I had only ever had 'the slipper' at Marston Road but I had watched Paul Moore once suffer the indignation of the cane - it was a humiliation from which I don't think he ever recovered.

"We have to go!" I yelled to John, thinking that the less late we were the less the punishment would be.

However, Trotter logic was very different and he replied matter-of-factly, "We're already late so we may as well stay." His peers shared the same philosophy and I was forced to wait. It was 11:15pm by the time the group had completed their encore, and we left trying to flag down a taxi.

We planned our excuse whilst the taxi driver drove us back. Basically, we had concocted a scenario where we had run for the bus, just missed it because the driver pulled off early. Then, we waited for the next bus and that didn't turn up, so we decided to join the taxi queue but there were many cab-loads before us because of the concert. We all synchronized our story and decided to stick to it, come what may.

When we arrived, hope against hope that we would be able to sneak straight into the dorm, Mr. Parker was stood with his arms folded at the main entrance. He pointed to the teachers' quarters and we were marched without sound into Mr. Hansen's room.

"Well?" demanded the headmaster. None of the others responded and the silence was overwhelming.

I cracked first and regurgitated our agreed excuse, while the others nodded along. I thought that I had represented our case well, and I even embroidered with vivid descriptions of our run for the early leaving bus, the extended wait for the bus-that-never-came and finally the huge queue at the taxi rank.

Hansen listened intently to my every word and then he turned to Barry Wise and simply said, "Barry?"

"The group didn't start till ten o'clock so we decided to stay, sir," he confessed, almost without conscience.

"Is this true?" he asked the others. They all-nodded in unison, as I was ludicrously shaking my head.

"Well, I appreciate your honesty, Cranston Roaders," said the headmaster in an ice-cold voice, "go to bed and we'll look at consequences in the morning."

I lay awake half the night, feeling gutted. Not only was I cast as the villain of the piece, I had dishonoured Marston Road, while the rest of the gang had emerged smelling of roses. By morning I had worked myself into such a state that I was anticipating a full witch-hunt with anti-Marstonians brandishing burning torches and demanding public flagellation. I felt so guilty that I would have flogged myself, at this point.

Anyway, all that happened was that Mr, Parker said, "I hope you dirty stop-outs enjoyed the concert because you are going to be peeling spuds all morning." Then he winked at me and all was right with the world again.

Even the potato peeling just involved washing the potatoes and then putting them in a big machine that peeled them for you. It was quite fun and it was apparent that the others had respect for me 'taking the rap' for them, even though it had never been my plan.

After we had eaten, our penance was over, and Mr. Hansen made a point of thanking me personally for helping prepare lunch. It was his way of letting me know that he had not held a grudge.

Later, we went to the pier and there was a ballroom with a juke box. I selected the brand-new Beatles song Yellow Submarine. It was not a song that you could dance to but it had a cracking chorus that everybody joined in. In fact, it went on to be a mantra for the rest of the holiday. Sonja found Fire Brigade by The Move and suddenly all the girls dropped their handbags to the ground and we were dancing. Then, I was only remembering the best part, of the best and worst day of my life.

The whole week could not have gone better, learning to dance, smoke, and talk normally to girls, were huge steps toward the new image I was trying to cultivate. Also, I was popular with the most notorious family in Hartley, which made me popular with the whole school. Even the teachers seemed to have forgiven my indiscretion.

However, nobody warns you about the downside to popularity: Jealousy! The son of the headmaster, Christopher Hansen, had been perfectly civil with me up until the Wednesday. However, on Thursday Morning, he approached me with a group of about six boys, who seemed aware of his intentions before me. Children of headteachers are in a tricky situation, in that they must avoid embarrassing their parent, but they need to prove themselves to their peers. Apparently, I provided his opportunity to score a few points.

Firstly, he stiffened his arms out in front of himself and his momentum was enough to launch me off my feet.

"Puff!" he yelled, which was a derogatory slant on my sexuality. This seemed ironic to me because I had some suspicions about his own sexual persuasion.

"Get off!" I responded, standing up and squaring up to him, raising my fists and adopting a boxing stance. My dad had taught Andrew and I how to box, after I had been bullied a few years prior. This seemed to surprise Hansen and the two dozen kids that were now forming a human boxing ring around us.

"Puff!" he said again, with slightly less gusto. I could tell that he had initially expected me to cower and submit. However, he did not know of the Wells philosophy. My dad's father had once trained him, with a slogan, "Never start a fight, son, but always be prepared to finish one." and suddenly I was weirdly fighting for three generations of family honour.

"Puff!" he called me for the third time, trying to grab me in a headlock. There are two types of playground fighters, the boxers and the wrestlers. I did not wrestle, that called for an upper body strength that I did not possess. Of course, Gary Roberts had proven that I could not box either, when he broke my nose twelve months prior, but he had caught me off guard, operating outside the Queensbury Rules of fisticuffs. So, when the headteachers son moved his arm around my neck, I poked an uppercut at his face and blood instantly appeared on his lip, as he reeled back. The crowd cheered which gave me confidence. At this, he charged me, head-butting me in the stomach and knocking the wind out of me. I can only imagine the entertainment for the crowd. It was School v School; Boxer v Wrestler; Puff v Heterosexual. As we gathered ourselves after the headbutt I could see that he was about to jump on top of me, which with his superior weight, would have pinned me into a position of submission. But he misjudged my speed and agility and as his torso lunged toward me I scooted sideways and landed another punch to his face. Again, the crowd yelled their approval. I jumped up and I saw Hansen make half an attempt to rise and then, with conscious effort he decided to stay down. I started walking away but a change of expression on the faces of the crowd directly in front of me, told me there was something going on behind me. I turned just in time to see the headmaster's son stand up and extend his right arm, but it was not to wrestle or punch, it was an offer of a handshake. I took his hand cautiously and we shook.

I thought about the whole surreal fight afterwards and realized that we had both won, just by participating in the fight, irrelevant of the victor.

I was quite shaken for the rest of the day and felt particularly vulnerable. But it felt good to win a fight as I had physically lost all my previous fights, even if I had had some moral victories. This was almost like a rite of passage, like getting 'jumped' into a gang.

By Friday, we knew the town of Douglas well. It was time to start trawling the souvenir shops for gifts for the family. For Andrew, I got this silver-coloured cigarette case with the famous three-legged emblem of the Isle of Man etched into it. Eric got a gonk, a little ugly baby-come-monster with sticking up bright yellow hair. Gonks were all the rage and I knew that Eric would love it. Dad's present was a stroke of genius. I knew that he loved kippers - the smelliest fish in the world, and many of the shops were advertising that they would ship special Isle of Man kippers free of charge to any destination. So, I arranged for them to send dad fresh kippers. If he didn't like them, I knew that Doodle would polish them off. However, Doodle deserved a present of his own and his was a no brainer. In the Isle of Man, years of feline in-breeding has resulted in cats having no tails. Literally, Manx cats have no more than a tiny stump where the tail should protrude. So, I was delighted to find a little Manx kitten fluffy toy, allegedly filled with irresistible cat attractant. Mum got an ashtray, with a picture of an Isle of Man tram. Even though nobody in the house smoked, since dad had given up for more than a year, she always had ashtrays for smoking visitors.

The trip back was very different than the one out. The Manx Maid glided across the stillest waters but we stayed on deck throughout and the tannoy appropriately blasted out, "My Ship is Coming In," by the Walker Brothers. We all smoked our final cigarettes, vowing to 'give it up' when we got back home. When we arrived back at Etruria station I was delighted to see that my dad was waiting on the platform, looking saner and suitably attired than when I left.

Chapter 3: They Think It's All Over!

Lonnie Donegan had been my favourite artist, back in the late 1950's, when I was still slurping Cod Liver Oil from a pre-licked spoon. I loved his classics like "My Old Man's a Dustman," and "Does Your Chewing Gum Lose its Flavour on the Bedpost Overnight?" However, the skiffle king did not belong on Radio 1 in 1966, in the times of cool bands like The Small Faces and The Hollies. Therefore, despite my passion for football, it was so annoying to turn on the radio and hear Tony Blackburn announce: "And still riding high in the charts, it's Mr Donegan singing about that little rascal, World Cup Willie."

"Dressed in red, white and blue, he's World Cup Willie
We all love him too, World Cup Willie......
(ad nauseum)"

Except for that fly in the ointment, July of 1966 was probably the best month of my entire life.

Not only had I finished Junior School and befriended the coolest kids in the whole of Staffordshire, it was also the month when England entertained the World Cup and football fever gripped the nation. Legendary players were on the television every night: Franz Beckenbauer the German midfield maestro; Pele, the undisputed World's greatest Brazilian genius; and then Eusebio, the Portuguese phenomenon.

The World Cup was nearly ruined before it started because somebody stole the famous Jules Rimet trophy. However, the public outrage must have shamed the thief because it was finally discovered under a bush, wrapped in newspaper, by a dog named Pickles.

Even as the host nation, England were not considered to be contenders, especially after a lukewarm 0-0 draw with Uruguay. At first, Brazil seemed to be in a league of their own. Every player on the team could interchange positions and they threw in tricks, just to entertain the crowd. They revolutionized the danger of free-kicks because they could bend the ball in mid-air, as if by magic. However, I learned that a football tournament of this nature was more of a 'marathon' than a 'sprint.'

It took more than glimmers of genius to grind out results and it was not necessarily the most entertaining team that won the contest. Scrappy defensive teams, like Argentina, could go just as far in the competition scoring by just a single goal in each game. Pele was injured early in the contest and

Brazil's bubble burst before the nation's eyes. Then there was North Korea, who were theoretical underdogs, who kept fluking so many goals that they were suddenly in the quarter-finals, set to face Eusebio's Portugal. The West Germans marched on with typical German consistency.

However, England remained under the radar until they met Argentina in the quarter-finals. Alf Ramsey, the quiet manager had kept the pressure off his players, while emphasizing the importance of team-work. Except for Bobby Charlton, who had the hardest shot in football, the England team had no world-famous names. The Argentinian team played dirty but, rather than intimidate the England team, it seemed to cement their resolve. Then the Argentine captain, named Ratin, was red-carded but refused to leave the field, which had the effect of consolidating the ever-growing patriotic fervour of the nation. Ramsey's boys were suddenly Ramsey's men.

Meanwhile, Eusebio's Portugal had a partial shock when the Koreans hammered three goals past them in the first half. However, that just fuelled the genius and it was 5-3 to Eusebio by the final whistle.

When we weren't watching football, we were playing. But it was no longer, "And its Pele on the wing,' it was more "Bobby Moore pushes it out to Nobby Stiles, who threads it through to Martin Peters," as we simulated our new heroes and all the England players became household names.

By the final, obviously against the unstoppable Germans, the country was as united as if they were back on the beaches of Dunkirk. The newspapers were tapping into wartime resentments, with Winston Churchill quotes that we would 'never surrender.'

Haller put the Germans ahead but then Hurst pulled one back with a splendid direct free kick. German penetration ran deep, as the English tried to bunker down but their blanket bombardment eventually paid off with a powerful shot, until the World's most controversial goal occurred. Hursty hit the underside of the bar with such force and backspin that the ball appeared to cross the goal line and spin out again. It seemed like an age before the referee finally agreed with what was obvious to every spectator in England. This brought the game to extra time, where Martin Peters scored a goal and Geoff Hurst put the game beyond dispute, as Kenneth Wolstenholme screamed the immortal lines, "There's some people on the pitch; they think it's all over - it is now!" The referee blew his final whistle. The next thing we knew, Bobby Moore was accepting 'Pickles find' from Queen Elizabeth and toothless Nobby Stiles was dancing his memorable jig around the field with the cup lofted high above his head.

A weird anti-climactic malaise descended on our household a couple of days after England's finest hour. I had been keeping a scrapbook of the whole event, which was now complete. We had been spoiled by the routine of nightly football piped into our living rooms and blanket coverage of the players and their families. Sudden withdrawal was like going cold turkey from a drug. The psychology of dealing with success was an entire different approach to recovering from disappointment. My parents decided that 'too much television" was the source of the depression and so they switched it off for August. I suppose that we had used up August's quota of television hours.

I switched on the radio, only to find the dreaded World Cup Willie song, still desecrating the airwaves. So, I decided to take my 5-year-old brother, Eric, for a walk and we ended up at a playground close to my school. Eric loved going to parks with me and he was straight on the swings, giving me directions on how to push him.

It seemed that we were alone but then I heard a voice behind me ask, "So is this your little brother, then?" It was Linda Harley, a girl from my class.

"No, it's my sister," I answered, using my new-found form of hilarity, sarcasm.

"Oh," she responded, taking a few seconds to absorb the humour, and then she smiled. Linda had long blonde wavy hair, a pre-Raphaelite nose and unusually green eyes. She looked different from when she was in the classroom and it took a while for me to identify that she was wearing make-up. Her hair smelled like sweet apples. I suddenly loved her hair and the fragrance seemed to drive my previous favourite girl smell, Sally Doyle's lavender soap, from its pole position in my olfactory memory banks.

"Do you miss, Marston Road?" I asked, just to make conversation. I was proud that I was not feeling the blushing sensation in my face that I usually experienced whenever a girl came near.

"No, I'm going to Brownhills in a month," she explained, nudging me out of the way, so that she could take over the swing-pushing duty. Brownhills was the girl's top high school in the city.

"I know, I'm going to Hartley High," I explained with a little symbiotic pride.

"Are you scared?" she asked, holding eye contact, so I had to tell the truth.

"Little bit," I replied. I wondered how I had sat opposite her so many times in class and not noticed the unique greenness of her eyes.

"Me too," she confided again showing me the importance of eye contact. I had had a 'lazy eye' when I was younger and people with lazy eyes tend to avoid the intimacy of prolonged eye contact. Luckily, I had outgrown the eye problem.

We were having some kind of a 'moment' because, inane as the conversation was, Eric's swing was now completely stationary and neither of us had noticed.

Then Linda said, "Does your sister want to go on the slide?" It took me a second to realize that she was also using sarcasm for our amusement.

When we left the park, we both agreed that we would be there the next day at around the same time. It was a loose arrangement but, by the time I got home, I realized that it was a 'date' in the loose sense of the word.

I was still riding high, feeling that I had overcome the shyness that had plagued my life and sweet apple smells filled my thoughts, when my mum summoned me to the kitchen with her, get-ready-for-a-good-hiding voice from my past.

I cowered, as I entered to see Eric sobbing uncontrollably.

Mum got right in my face and said, "Martin did you call your brother a girl?"

"No," I responded.

"Well why's he crying his little heart out and saying that you told some girl that he was a girl? she demanded.

Then it came back to me, "Oh I was joking," I explained, "she asked if he was my brother and I said, 'No it's my sister' just to be funny.

"Well how's that funny? You've broke his little heart!" she said.

"It was just a joke," I retorted, feeling that the whole episode was being blown out of proportion.

"I'm sorry Eric, it was just a joke. Nobody thinks you're a girl," I assured him.

"That girl does," he sobbed.

"No, she doesn't, she was just joking, too," I explained. It occurred to me that sarcasm was a trickier tool in the comedy pallet than I first thought.

I apologized again, and saw mum's mood subside, and then she asked the question that was obviously fuelling her curiosity, "So who's this girl?"

"Nobody" I replied.

"That's a funny name for a girl," my mum teased, trying her own hand at sarcasm.

"Can I put the radio on?" I asked to divert the topic.

"Of course," mum responded, realizing that she was making me feel uncomfortable. The radio must have been listening because when I switched it on it was in the middle of an aptly sarcastic song by "The Who:"

"I'm a boy, I'm a boy!" sang Roger Daltrey and Pete Townsend in strained harmony. It was hilarious and even Eric saw the funny side.

Chapter 4: Day Tripper.

When the scarily eccentric Jimmy Saville introduced The Beatles, singing 'Day Tripper,' on Top of the Pops, we were not to know that this would be their final appearance on the show. George's twanging guitar riff was an instant classic, although the lyrics seemed somewhat nonsensical. I thought that the song was about falling in love, with a girl who had omitted to mention that she was only in town for twenty-four hours. However, my dad said that it contained secret drug references; I refused to entertain such wicked lies about my heroes.

The song title inspired my mum, to suggest that we boys should plan a day trip.

"Where can we go?" I asked, looking for guidance.

"You're all high school students," she responded, giving me a half-wink, "you're old enough to make your own plans."

So, Tony Boswell, Barry Pratt, Andrew and I met in my dad's garage to discuss a destination. We unanimously agreed on the mystically named Thor's Cave, in Manifold Valley. The next morning, I was put in charge of food and made enough cheese and Branston Pickle sandwiches to feed an army. They were then equally distributed between the four saddle bags.

Tony conducted a mechanical check of all our bikes: tire inflation; seat height; handlebar adjustment; he oiled my chain and replaced a worn rubber brake block. Finally, he checked that his puncture outfit had all the items necessary for emergency repairs.

Andrew consulted Tony Boswell's map to Manifold Valley. Andrew calculated that, even with my 3-geared bike we could average ten miles an hour. Since the cave was only seventeen miles away, if we took the shortest route, we should be there in less than two hours.

Barry Pratt had checked the weather forecast and confirmed that it was going to be glorious, which was not a word that he would have made up. As predicted, the sun was up early and so, unburdened by excessive clothes, we took off in T-shirts and shorts.

Andrew's route took us along some minor roads through Cellarhead and Froghall. Unfortunately, the map never really told us about the steep hills that we were facing. Admittedly, we probably hit 20 mph on the way down but there seemed to be more ups than downs and the inclines were so fierce that we had to dismount and push the bikes half the way. As a result, we took nearly four hours to get to the little village of Grindon, at the top of the valley.

We were all starving by then, and decided that we would find a shady spot to eat our hard-earned lunch. Tony discovered that the door to the church in Grindon was open. There was nobody inside and he persuaded us that churches always left their doors open, in case anybody wanted to go in and pray. So, we took a pew each and gobbled down our sandwiches, which turned out to be only just enough to satiate our tiny army of four. Unfortunately, I had not thought to pack drinks and we were all simultaneously gasping for fluid.

"I know," echoed Barry's voice, as he disappeared out of the front door. One minute later, he returned with two bottles of richly creamed milk, that he had spotted on someone's front doorstep. We guzzled down half a bottle each. We drank so quickly that we could feel it curdling with the Branston in our stomachs. It suddenly seemed like sacrilege to be drinking stolen milk in a church and it felt like we were invoking the wrath of God, manifesting in the form of nausea.

We sped quickly down into the valley and spotted Thor's cave. Leaving the bikes at the foot of the hill, we climbed up to the cave. It was an optical illusion really because we kept feeling like we were there but the climb was long and strenuous. However, when we arrived at the cave we were not disappointed. It went back further than we thought and some of the channels ran deep. Luckily, the ever-practical Tony had thought to bring his flashlight. After a few screams, and echoed "Hellos, Andrew decided we should play a game. We each had to sing an appropriate song.

He started, with a song that had recently been a hit for Los Bravos.

"Black is black, I want my baby back," his voice echoed around the cave. We all cheered in appreciation, and to hear our own echoes. It occurred to me that he had contrived the game and that there was no other relevant song.

However, then Tony had a brilliant response, with a Rolling Stones song, "Have you seen your mother baby, standing in the shadows!" We all clapped and whistled at this spontaneous genius, and even Andrew voted that it surpassed his own effort. The pressure was now on Barry and myself. Barry seemed flummoxed but then a huge smile came across his face as a Lee Dorsey hit came to him.

"Workin' in a coalmine," he sang, and we all joined in, "going down, down, down, Workin' in a coal mine, Oops, about to slip down." Andrew, who was now the self-appointed judge decided that it was a dead heat with Tony's effort.

"*Great,*" my sarcastic-self thought, "*that means I'm going to be in last place.*" I wracked my brains but it was obvious that there could not possibly have been more than three hits relating to caves. I thought of "Strangers in the Night" but I knew that it would not draw more than a polite chuckle. I even drew breath to launch into Frank Sinatra's classic when inspiration hit me. It was a Simon and Garfunkel classic, recently recorded by The Bachelors, called The Sound of Silence.

"Hello darkness, my old friend," I sang.

"Brill," said Barry, and then they all whistled and cheered. Everyone looked to Andrew for the thumbs up, or down. I was convinced that he would find a way to make me lose, such was our sibling rivalry. However, he was looking at me with admiration.

He declared, "We have a winner! Mart!" It was a wonderful and rare sensation, to have my elder brother give me public approval and I felt wonderfully proud in that moment.

Unfortunately, I had very little time to savour the moment before a pressing issue presented itself. I was suddenly wishing we had taken a little more digesting time after our lunch and creamy milk. I suddenly had a lactose-intolerant call of nature and there were no toilets in the cave. So, we had to start a premature descent and seek out a suitable bush to squat behind. Luckily, I had saved the grease-proofed paper that had recently wrapped my cheese and Branston sandwich. It was barely adequate under the circumstances but the Lord had a final trick up his sleeve. As I was carefully manoeuvring to avoid stepping in my own ghastly deposits, a flash of lightning and an almighty thunderbolt hit a tree less than fifty feet away. If I had not just evacuated my alimentary canal, I think that would have done it. I leapt up, pulling up my shorts and met the other three, who all looked decidedly pale.

As we ran down the path, the Heaven's really seemed to open, and we were literally running down a stream by the time we got back to our bikes.

"It's just a short storm," Barry assured us.

"Where did you get the weather forecast from, Barry?" Tony asked, as we pedalled along the valley. We expected him to say, the Evening Sentinel, which was renowned for its unreliability. But it was worse than that.

"My dad said it would be nice all day!" he admitted.

We all groaned in unison because everyone knew Barry's dad was not a weather forecaster, he was a prize idiot! Even Barry knew that.

Having realized the flaw in the Froghall route, Tony had already decided that our best return home a slightly longer but flatter road through Leek. First, we had to get to the main road, as we rode along the valley until we came to a place called Waterhouses. We would normally have laughed at the irony but unfortunately, the warm rain with which God had initially teased us, was suddenly cold and almost like a sheet of water. We knew of the dangers of sheltering under trees during a thunderstorm so we decided the safest thing to do was to keep riding;

Tony shouted, "Rubber tyres will insulate us!"

Andrew retorted, "Wood's an insulator but it doesn't bloody stop the lightning from ripping apart an Oak tree.

They both had a point. However, Andrew's knowledge was all theoretical, so I preferred to believe the ever-practical Tony. However, the terror of being frazzled by lightning seemed to be soon superseded by the threat of hypothermia. As we pedalled through an arctic version of the bowels of Hell, I really cursed that I had relied on a tee-shirt and shorts for my only protection against the elements.

"If we ride faster, we won't get as wet!" shouted Barry. It made sense to me.

Andrew again countered with alternative logic, "The faster you ride the more raindrops to hit, you fool!" That made sense to me, too. Not that it mattered because my leg muscles were so numb with fatigue and cold that pedalling faster wasn't really an option.

Finally, we reached the outskirts of Leek but there was still an incline to negotiate. Everyone else dropped to first gear and tackled the slope but I just dropped my bike on the floor and began to bawl unabashedly. All the freshly acquired status of being an eleven-plus passer, girl-dating, friend-of-the-Trotters evaporated. My spirit was broken as I watched the other three bikes disappear up the hill and around the bend. Then, as if to rub electrons into an open wound, God sent another terrifying thunderclap to zap a wooden tree, right next to the metal Bradnop sign, less than a hundred feet in front of me. It was if he was showing contempt for the rules of insulators and conductors.

"Bloody Hell Fire!" I whimpered, as the moment turned surreal. If ever there was a need for a guardian angel, it was at that moment and miraculously, a voice echoed my own.

"Bloody Hell Fire! "came Barry Pratt's familiar voice. "I think you could be right, mate. I think we nettled the Almighty Thor in his cave. I don't think he likes The Bachelors."

Apparently, when he noticed that I was no longer with the group, he had turned around and ridden back to look for me. Barry had been my best friend from the age of five. We had forged an empathetic bond that was almost magical, in our younger days, when we used to play fantasy games with a toy teddy bear and panda. There were times when we would get so engrossed in our games that we became totally detached and oblivious to the real world. We were always rescuing one another from head-shrinking natives, or gangs of teddy-boys or anything that our imaginations could conjure up. So, his voice instantly comforted me.

"Bloody Hell Fire!" we repeated in unison, as we contemplated the charred tree.

"Leek's just around the corner," Barry told me, "come on, we can walk our bikes."

"Okay," I obeyed, picking up my bike by its sludgy handlebars.

And so, we trudged step by step up the ever-steepening bend, and Barry kept a running commentary going, just like when we were young kids, again.

"And the soldiers are returning from the battle, exhausted but victorious," he said, as he set a steady marching pace. "War-torn and bedraggled, as the crowds line the streets of Leek, waiting to greet them in the pouring rain."

I took over the commentary, "Every woman clutches a union jack, hoping against hope, that her man has survived the battle."

"Hoping the soldiers still have all their limbs," added Barry.

"Hoping the Privates, still have their privates," I joked.

This cracked us both up and we broke down into fits of giggles. It suddenly seemed to both of us that it was the funniest joke that had ever been said. The laughter distracted us from the hypothermia and delirium and, in no time, we were marching hysterically into the town centre where Andrew and Tony were sheltering in a shop doorway. This was not quite the anticipated flag-waving women but a welcome sight, nonetheless.

"Where've you been?" asked Andrew, looking confused by our hysteria.

"We just nearly got struck by lightning!" I exaggerated.

"It set a tree on fire!" Barry added to the story.

"You're kidding," said Andrew with incredulity. He seemed more concerned at having missed a spectacle than nearly losing a brother.

Barry and I tucked into the shop doorway with the other two as we contemplated our next move. Tony explained that we were still eight miles from home, the first of which was all uphill. The good news was that, now that we had found shelter, the downpour stopped, as quickly as it had originally started. Tony suggested that I try and get some water out of my tee shirt, so I took it off and he rung it out for me, using his vice-like grip, that had crushed many a hand with his party-piece handshake. It almost felt worse when I put it back on but the fact that we had a plan was somewhat reassuring.

So, we set off down Leek Road, with the sun on our backs and the wind behind us. Soon we were dismounting for the epic trudge up the notoriously endless Leek bank, knowing that every painful step brought us closer to the top of the hill. The marching army in my head turned to French foreign legionnaires forging forward, with jellied legs fighting the sand dunes, desperately trying to forget the unrequited loves of my life, Sally Doyle and now Linda Harley. False peaks toyed with my spirit. I looked up at Barry and imagined him in a similar world, or maybe leading his horse through the apache-encrusted mountains of cowboy country. Any focus was better than the cramping lactic acid pangs.

Finally, against all hope, we reached the top of the massive incline and our arrival was heralded by another of nature's marvels. A giant double rainbow arched the distant highway and we rode once more into a cascade of raindrops. As gruelling as the climb had been, the elation of whizzing down the other side was exhilarating. The 'second wind' carried us for the next few miles until less than a mile from home, the 'second wall' hit us all simultaneously. Even with the rain to mask their tears, I could see that Andrew and Tony had reached the same emotional point that the Bradnop thunderclap had induced in me. My two heroes were going down into the emotional abyss, with which I was all too familiar. For my own protection, as much as anything, I had to use every resource at my disposal to avoid witnessing this.

As always, I tried to use humour to salvage the situation. I told them a joke that I had heard John Trotter tell when we were in the Isle of Man.

"What's the difference between a cross-eyed hunter and a constipated owl"? I asked.

I knew they had heard me but nobody responded.

I repeated the conundrum, "What is the difference between a cross-eyed hunter and a constipated owl?"

"I don't bloody know!" snarled Andrew, "what is the sodding difference?"

"One shoots and can't hit," I explained, "and the other hoots and can't shit!"

Barry laughed openly and his laughter brought a smirk to Andrew and Tom's face. So, I gave them the other joke that Kenny Trotter had told us.

"What's the difference between a bumpy road and a nymphomaniac?" I asked.

"Don't know?" said Andrew, a little less aggressively.

"One knackers your tires," I revealed. I did not even have to say the other part as a metaphorical light bulb went off over their heads.

They yelled in unison, "And the other tires your knackers!" It worked, all our spirits lifted enough for us to pedal home.

When we arrived, the heavens really opened, mum and dad were so relieved to see us that they greeted us with chastisement, in true parent fashion.

"Where the bloody Hell have you been?" dad shouted, "Your mother's been worried sick!" This was his way of saying that he had also been concerned but dad struggled with demonstrating affection.

I looked over at mum and she was welling up, "You daft buggers," she said, swallowing back the tears. "Your dad's put the emersion heater on; you both need a hot bath." She could see that Andrew was trying to retain his dignity, fighting the urge to cry. Her eyes motioned to the stairs, "You first, trouble," she told him. Andrew fled for the door, glad of the chance to conceal his feelings from us.

Without the same commitment to pride, physical and emotional exhaustion consumed me and I began to shiver and shake, almost to the point of convulsion.

"You, poor baby," said mum, taking a towel and wrapping it around me, and clutching me tightly. I would normally have pulled away from her, with my descending adolescence, but she was right. High schooler or not, I was a poor baby. I began to cry, just like a baby.

"Let's get this fire going," said dad, working a piece of coal with the poker, to hide his embarrassment. "You'll be okay, son," he whispered, with a slight quiver in his own voice, "you'll be okay."

Chapter 5: Prestatyn Holiday Camp

Dad must have been Britain's most mediocre gambler because, whenever my mum asked him how he had fared at the bookies, he would always answer, "Just broke even, dear." This was the only safe response because, if he lost even a morsel of the family budget he would be considered irresponsible, but by winning he would be expected to share the spoils.

One day in August he had a four-way accumulator bet, commonly known as a 'Yankee' come in, and before he could harness his excitement he made an announcement to the family.

"I've just won a hundred and fifty quid on an each-way Yankee!" he spluttered.

"Great, let's go to Butlin's," my mum suggested, without hesitation.

Dad looked over at Eric, who was the direct result of the previous Butlin's trip. Then he looked over at me and stated that, "Martin's only just had a holiday!"

"Well, they all need new uniforms and shoes for school," mum countered. Her psychology worked perfectly because, painful as it was to part with his freshly acquired riches, he sure as hell would rather spend it on a holiday than school uniforms.

"Tell you what, we'll go to Prestatyn Holiday Camp, as long as we don't have to see your sister," dad compromised. Mum agreed, even though her sister lived less than a mile from the camp, and Prestatyn was really considered a 'poor man's Butlin's.' The holiday camp concept was launched in the late 1950's as the affordable working man's holiday. Prestatyn had managed to cheapen it further.

The Beach Boys belted out "God only knows, what I'd be without you," on the tannoy, as our Sunbeam Rapier drew into Great Britain's most affordable holiday camp.

The Sunbeam Rapier was a symbol of our family's social climb, fuelled mainly by the death of

Grandpa Eric a year earlier. Suddenly my Nana Lena had inherited more wealth than she could handle and she gave the Sunbeam Rapier to my dad. She also promised to give him the twenty percent deposit to buy a house, once Eric's estate had sorted out.

"At least it's sunny," dad announced, and instantly The Kinks song, Sunny Afternoon, came on the tannoy. We all laughed at the ironic timing and I felt like music was specifically playing a subconscious score to my life.

Dad seemed initially disappointed at the camp, which he perhaps saw as below our newfound social standing.

"I like the cheapness but I don't like the cheapness, if you know what I mean," he philosophized, as he parked outside the Reception area.

"I'm not going to waste a brain cell on that one," said mum, realizing the compendium of ironies was best kept boxed. When it came to courting misery, mum and dad never needed much encouragement. But dad never stayed down for long and after a few minutes in the reception area, he came out clutching a downstairs chalet key.

"I knew our luck was in!" he told mum. She was still nonplussed but she seemed to 'come around' when she saw that there was a door between the children's room and their main bedroom.

"Better than Butlin's," insisted dad, presumably referring to the fact that their family chalets only had alcoves and recesses to accommodate the bunk beds.

There first move was to throw Andrew and I our swimming trunks and send us off to the Olympic-sized swimming pool. It was hard to imagine that an Olympic pool was only 25-yards long but we took them at their word. Unfortunately, the 'Miss Prestatyn Holiday Camp' competition was taking place around the pool and so we were not allowed to go in the water. However, we were both developing a mild interest in what adults considered beauty, so we decided to stay and spectate. There were twelve bikini-clad 'beauties,' each with a large circular wrist-card displaying a number, being paraded in front of a boisterous crowd. Apparently, it was most important to crown the Beauty Queen on the first day because she would be carrying the sceptre for the whole week.

There were only one of the twelve finalists, who had a pretty face and that was *Seven*. I was amazed when my choice was ignored in favour of *Five* - a big breasted, round-bottomed woman with fat lips, peroxide hair and a piggy nose. After the swimsuit and high-heels walk around the pool, each woman was asked the same question:

"If you won the hundred pounds' prize what would you do with it" asked the compere, Bob the Blue Coat.

"Well Bob, I'd give it to the woman who brought me into this world," said the red-headed *One*. A few of the older women 'Ahhhhh...ed' appreciatively but it was not an answer that inspired the raunchy male majority.

"The midwife, then?" shouted a loudmouth. The inebriated multitude erupted with laughter.

The fair-skinned *One* had obviously misjudged the amount of sun-exposure to which she would be subjected because she was already lobster pink and the contest had a long way to go.

"I wouldn't give it to the mid-wife. Looks like she dropped you in the boiling water!" shouted the same heckler, once again to rapturous applause.

"I'd spend it on a bathful of calamine lotion, if I were her," I whispered to Andrew, who was tickled by my commentary.

Two, who according to Andrew, 'was brave to show herself in a bikini,' tried to play to the crowd's ebullience She had a different use for the prize money. She declared, "Well Bob, I'd buy everyone here a drink."

A few members of the audience screamed their appreciation but as the cheer began to subside, a comedian shouted, "You'd have to buy me more than one drink, love!" The mob went wild with laughter, and *Two* ended up redder than *One*.

It all seemed unnecessarily cruel to me but Andrew pointed out that public ridicule was a risk they took when they entered the 'vanity contest.'

Three would have been my second choice, until she tried to answer the question with an excruciating stammer, " W-w-w-w-well, B-B-B-B-Bob," she started to answer.

Bob's comedic instinct overshadowed any empathy, as he mocked, "N-n--not s-s-s-so --b-b-bad, a-a-and y-y-your-s-s-self?" He turned to the audience for approval but, even a drunken hoard drew the line at this level of satire.

Some of the revellers booed but it was impossible to say whether their derision was aimed at stammering *Three* or Bob. *Three* would have been justified in avoiding further speech but instead she started her answer again, "W-w-w-well B-B-Bob," she said, slightly better than before.

Bob interrupted again, "Hey *Contestant Three*, we have a tradition here at Prestatyn Holiday Camp," he turned and winked at the audience. "Every competitor has to recite a tongue-twister. Repeat after me: Peter Piper picked a peck of pickled pepper. Where's the peck of pickled peppers Peter Piper picked?"

Andrew and I gasped at Bob's wickedness; it was like watching an accident from which it was impossible to look away.

We watched in disbelief as *Three* seemed up for the challenge. She drew a deep breath and said "P-P-P-Piss off, Bob!" She accompanied this with an unambiguous two-fingered gesture. We all cheered as Bob got his comeuppance.

"Disqualified!" yelled Bob, suddenly losing his sense of insensitivity.

Three turned to the audience and shouted, "W-w-where she-sh-should B-B-Bob s-s-stick his p-p-prize money?"

"Up his arse!" they replied as one voice. It was brilliant, absolutely brilliant.

Four had no chance. The crowd spent her interview discussing *Three's* exit and nobody even heard her plan to donate her unlikely winnings to Cancer research. Furthermore, she had no deportment and spent the entire interrogation with one hand over her boobs and the other over her stomach. She could not wait to get out of the limelight and neither could the audience. She was lucky that Bob was still nursing his wounds because he let her pass without humiliation. But Bob was not down for long, and as timid *Four* returned to a life of obscurity, Bob gave a double shrug of the shoulders and his fully obnoxious personality was restored.

In contrast to *Four, Five* 'owned' the stage once she got the mike in her hand; everything she said seemed to have double meaning.

"So, tell me Contestant Number *Five*, have you met Mike?" he said, handing her the microphone.

"Well hello, Mike," she said in a Diana Dors-like sexy voice. She ran her fingers erotically around the microphone, leaving little to the imagination, much to the delight of the crowd.

Bob leaned over, and asked the next question, "So how would you use the hundred quid?"

"Well Bob," she continued in her bedroom voice, "I've always been an animal lover." She took a deep breath so that her heaving cleavage almost popped out of her bikini top.

"I bet you are," joked Bob in a lascivious voice, "I can see you've bought a couple of puppies with you." The last statement only made sense in Bob's head but we all cheered anyway.

"So, as an 'animal lover' what would you do with the money?" Bob repeated.

She turned to the judges, licked her lips and said, "I would release the beast in you."

It was nonsensical but from the way the crowd whistled it was obvious that the competition was basically over.

Bob gleaned from the next five, including my favourite *Seven,* that they would do something boring with the money, rudely rallying them along with a "Blah, blah, blah, blah!"

By the time *Eleven* had seen the first ten, she was obviously having second thoughts about subjecting herself to Bob's contemptuous comments. She tried to storm off, much to her husband's dismay. He obviously had plans for the winnings and tried to coax her back onto the stage. The coax turned to a shove, which evolved into a tussle, ending up with them both going in the pool.

"Yes!" shouted the crowd, who had been suffering a lull. That livened things up because the humiliation sent her into total rage. She seemed to acquire a freakish strength and she held his head under the water. It was funny at first but then it started to look more serious. We were potentially witnessing an attempted murder and half the crowd held their breath in empathy.

"She's killing him," shouted Bob, and sure enough the two life-guards, who had been enjoying the break from their job, had to dive in and pull the woman off her husband.

He gasped, along with the more empathetic witnesses, as he finally got his face out of the water. It took a dozen breaths to replenish his haemoglobin with enough oxygen to speak. However, the whole crowd could see Eleven's fierce face and they sensed that, if he said the wrong words at this point, he was going under again.

"Sorry," he said. She moved toward him and put her arms around his neck and kissed him. He had picked the right word and redeemed himself, much to the relief of the crowd.

Finally, *Twelve* stepped up, and virtually eliminated her chances by telling Bob she would spend the money on a horse.

"You mean you'd bet it on a horse? asked the confused comedian.

"No, I would buy a horse for riding," she told them. Since more people at the camp had eaten horse than ridden one, nobody identified with her ambitions.

"You can ride me, if you like, love!" yelled the uncouth heckler.

"Ay, enough of that," declared Bob, suddenly manifesting another mood from his palate - righteous indignation.

The ten remaining contestants were asked to 'strut their stuff' twice around the pool, to the music of Manfred Mann, singing Pretty Flamingo, whilst the judges pretended to deliberate on the merits of each of the competitors. Then, to nobody's surprise, *Five* was called to the stage to receive her crown, cheque, and a list of duties for the week.

The Prestatyn Princess (and her puppies) first duty was to open the "Bop till You Drop "opening night dance. By coincidence, it was one of the judges who was selected to accompany the beauty queen, as a Bill Hayley and the Comet's song from the 1950's directed them to 'Rock around the clock.' Andrew and I were disappointed that the first dance we had ever attended was dedicated to primitive teddy boy music from the last decade. On the other hand, dad was in his element. In no time, he and mum got up and began to rock and twirl, matching the best of the dancers.

Andrew and I wandered around, trying to cadge cigarettes off the Rothman's promotional girls. They each carried a tray of cigarettes, like that used by the choc ice ladies of the cinemas. They were sophisticated looking women, dressed like air hostesses and offering free cigarettes and matches to everyone who walked past. Everyone, except me and my brother.

Mum and dad were literally 'having a ball' until the compere put on some smoochy music and announced a Gentleman's Excuse Me. That meant that men could tap each other on the shoulder, and this initiated the woman being passed to the tapper, to complete the dance. True to the spirit, dad went and tapped *Seven,* from the earlier beauty contest, as the singer sang, "Put your head on my shoulder, hold me in your arms, baby." I thought that it was interesting that dad and I were both attracted to the same pretty face but I was also a little distressed that he had abandoned mum in the middle of the dance floor.

So, I went over to her and said, "Excuse me, may I have the pleasure of this dance?"

Mum sniffed back the incipient tears and forced a smile, responding, "Of course, young man."

We sort of rocked back and forth from foot to foot, as she waited for me to take the lead. I had no clue how to do that and her whispered instructions of "Left, right together. Right, left together," were no help. However, it was not a problem for long because I now got a tap on my shoulder. I hoped that it was dad but it was actually a handsome Blue Coat, who knew exactly how to lead. I was uncomfortable placing my mum in the arms of a charming Adonis but it could have been worse - it could have been Bob! Dad scampered back to mum at the end of the song, seemingly jealous. I kept myself entertained watching the dynamic for the rest of the evening. *Seven's* eyes were fixed on dad for most of the night, while mum checked *Seven's* status intermittently. Dad's focus was to perpetually shield eye contact between mum and the Blue Coat Adonis.

At 9 pm, when the chalet child-minding service ended, we took over Eric-watching duties. He was so deeply asleep that he never noticed the changing of the guards. Nor did he stir when mum and dad crept noisily in two hours later.

Mum giggled, "Shush, you'll wake the children," which jerked me from a romantic dream I was having about *Seven*. The commotion and frustration, caused me to fidget, which then awakened Andrew, in the bunk below. Eric slept on.

"Another little brother coming up!" Andrew joked. I laughed out of politeness, then I puzzled over it for about five minutes before I got what he was implying.

"Oh, I get it!" I declared, rather too loudly.

"Go to sleep!" mum and dad yelled in synchronized tone. I tried desperately to get back to my dream with *Seven* but she was gone forever.

The next couple of days consisted of minding Eric, in the amusement arcade, playing the slot machines, bingo and the penny tilt machines. We were in there for so long that we learned the idiosyncrasies of all the contraptions. I found that, with a few strategic nudges I could boost my winnings at about the same speed that I was feeding it to the slot machines. I contemplated the irony that I was 'just breaking even.'

"All or Nothing" by the Small Faces was my favourite song and it seemed to be playing regularly on the speakers in the amusement arcade. This fuelled my theory that my life was indeed foreshadowed by the music industry.

Then, Andrew discovered a teen's play room, with a full-size table tennis table, quarter size snooker table and a dart board. It was all we needed. It was irrelevant that the sun shone all week, and we missed the donkey derby, knobbly knees competition and glamorous granny contest, Andrew and I just played and played ping pong, hour on hour. At first, we were constantly trying to beat one another, so every stroke of the bat was intended to be the killer shot. The result was very short rally's. Basically, Andrew either won the game, when his killer shots went in or lost the game, when his killer shots hit the net or went out. Either way, it was not much fun for me, as I felt like a mere foil. So, we changed the motivation; once Andrew began to get bored we started to count how many times we could keep the rally going. At first, it was hard to get more than twenty but then we got into a rhythm. As we got flowing, twenty became fifty and then a hundred. Then, we got Eric counting for us, which he was happy to do. Between the bingo and score keeping Eric was getting quite a mathematical education. As we worked together we developed a serious psychic alignment and then we started to hit the ball a little harder, and impose a little more top spin, countered by bottom spin.

By the Thursday, my mum sent dad in to drag us out because she felt like we were not getting value for money, spending so much time cooped up in a small room. However, dad was thrilled to see his sons mastering his favourite game and, by the time mum came to check what the delay had been, she discovered him, with his sweater off, coaching the three of us. Even Eric had been absorbing some of the ball-eye coordination instincts as he counted our hits. Dad was thrilled that his youngest could already paddle the ball back, as he set him up.

"Kids a genius, Bet," dad explained to mum.

"Palest genius, I ever saw," she retorted like there was a logical connection between suntan and intelligence, "The kids need some sun, Peter!"

When mum's insistence finally got us out of the recreation room, we all went for a family walk out of the Holiday Camp and onto the beach. Our barefoot walk would have been fine, except that there happened to be an invasion of jellyfish, at the time. Literally, the stinging coelenterates were all over the beach at 2 foot intervals. It was rumoured that a sting from one of these creatures could paralyze you, although dad insisted that it was no worse than a bee sting. I was particularly nervous but, as usual, Andrew had to invent a competition.

"Let's race to the next breaker," he insisted. "Ready, steady, go!"

I never needed a second invite to race. Andrew knew that I could easily outrun him and my agility was probably superior. Indeed, we had had similar races down 'Dog Shit Lane,' a poo-riddled street on the way to Stoke City's football ground, and Andrew had lost when literally 'the shit hit the fan' (football fan). Therefore, I was confident that I could win the race to the sand breaker. In fact, I was winning comfortably until Andrew yelled, "Don't step on one, they're poisonous!"

At that very moment, there was suddenly a clump of jellyfish right ahead. I had a choice, I could shorten my stride and aim at the space between them, or I could leap over all of them. Unfortunately, I did a hybrid manoeuvre and ended with a knee in the middle of one splodgy creature and a hand smack dab in the middle of another.

"Ahhhhh!" I screamed in anticipation of the pain. Then, "Ahhhhhhhhhhh!" I screamed again, as the anticipated pain took fruition. Agony shot into my leg. Somehow the handful of jelly had left me unscathed but the knee felt like someone had stabbed it with an ice-pick. This was not like a bee sting, it was the precursor to paralysis. I looked down, and I could see that the place where the stinger had entered my knee was beginning to swell. I felt myself tearing up, as the combination of pain and fear took a grip of me. I felt the pain climbing up my leg and turning from agony to numbness.

"I'm going to be paralyzed aren't I?" I wept.

"Should have left 'em playing table tennis, dad told mum."

"Peter," mum snapped back, "your son could be paralyzed and you're more interested in being right!"

"I am going to be paralyzed?!" I reminded them. Not that they were listening to me.

"Oh, no dear, we all know who's always right and it's never me, is it?" he sarcastically responded. "Maybe he can still play paraplegic table tennis." I lost my admiration for sardonic humour, now. I could not believe that they were turning the worst moment of my life into a petty argument.

"Am I going to be paralyzed?" I demanded. I began to wonder if they'd still let me go to Hartley High School without any feeling in my lower body.

"Don't be daft," dad reassured me, "It's just a bee sting."

"It was a jellyfish," I reminded him.

"It's all the same thing," dad calmly explained.

Andrew looked scared and decided to explain the science of the situation, "It's just your body over-reacting to a foreign protein."

"You have to 'suck it out!' declared my big brother."

The numbness was still spreading, and I suddenly had another fear.

"My dick's going to be paralyzed!" I screamed. This added a new dimension of terror. I was starting to acquire some affection for my own 'little Pete' and I was not happy at the thought of never feeling those sensations again. I tried to reach my mouth to my knee but it suddenly seemed like it was the only part of my body that I could not reach. Then, Andrew became hero, he leapt on the swelling and bit and sucked and spit all in one movement.

"Ahhhhhhhh!" I screamed, as I saw blood in the phlegm ball that hit the sand.

"I think I got it!" he reassured me. "You'll be fine now."

It was hard to calculate how much his action had saved me and how much was psychological but I felt a little better and the numbness slowly begun to be replaced with pain.

"Better?" he asked?

"Better," I responded. I mean it was still sore but I almost welcomed the pain, over the alternative of paralysis.

"I couldn't let my little brother have a paralyzed dick!" he smiled, causing me to blush and grin at the same time.

"Andrew!" mum chastised. It was mum's way to displace her fears with a display of anger. I could see that she had been scared because her eyes were moist.

"Really?" Andrew responded, shaming both my parents into silence.

When we got back inside the safety of the camp Andrew asked if we could return to the games

70

room. Mum and dad put up no resistance and that's where we spent the rest of the holiday.

It had apparently been a gloriously sunny week, even though we had spent most of it indoors. However, as we were leaving the skies began to cloud up. Of course, the song that was broadcast across the tannoy's airwaves as we were leaving, was the Walker Brothers singing, "The Sun Ain't Gonna Shine, Anymore."

Chapter 6: The Ice Cream Wars

The first day at Hartley High School was magical. Of course, I had been hearing all the stories from Andrew and Barry for a couple of years, but it was hard to imagine that it would live up to the myths. Having a brother in the school was both a blessing and a curse. It was an advantage to have a brother who was popular, in the school, because it gave me an instant friendship group. It also prepared me, so that I was not quite such a 'lamb to the slaughter' as the other First Years.

For instance, the uniform list that parents used, stated that all pupils must have a Hartley High School cap and that First Years were expected to wear grey shorts. I was so relieved that Andrew had persuaded my mum to ignore the Chawners salesman, who took the trouble to measure my head for my cap-fitting.

"His brother said that nobody wears the caps," my mum affirmed.

"I believe that the school is going to be reinstating the tradition this year, madam." insisted the smarmy salesman.

"Nobody ever wears them!" Andrew reiterated, "you'd have to be crazy!"

On the first day, most First Years, or 'fags' as they called us, never got their caps as far as school. Cap-snatching was an initiation and the majority of fag-caps were unceremoniously launched from the school bus windows, by the bullies. I even grabbed one myself and threw it over my shoulder for the back-seat smokers to use as an ashtray.

A bigger mistake than the caps, were the short trousers that Chawners snuck into their itinerary. Exposed legs wreaked of mollycoddling. If only the over-zealous parents had realized the damage would take years to undo. They obviously did not have elder brothers to guide them through the faux-pas of high school survival.

School toilets were the most dangerous place. Firstly, Andrew had warned me to take a good look around before using the communal urinal. It was fair game to creep up behind you, midstream, and give you a firm nudge. With both hands pre-occupied, it was easy to end up with pee all over your trousers, or even the trousers of the person peeing next to you.

If care was taken for number one's, it was unwise to plan any number twos at school. The toilets were an unsavoury place and a gathering spot for smokers. It was a common practice for smokers to lob their lit butt ends over the door of any closed cubicle. A glowing fag-end was not a welcome addition to the lap of a toilet squatter. They were also known to throw water or gob over the doors. Even if nothing happened, the intimidation factors involved in finding yourself behind a toilet door made defecation strictly an emergency game.

If bullies operated *in cognito* in the toilets, it was blatantly part of the lunchroom regime. In some perverse attempt to get an equal blending of the year groups at the tables, the eight seat tables were first settled by two sixth form servers. Then four upper school kids were let in, saving the foot of the table for the second and first years.

The servers removed the lids and served out potatoes, meat and vegetables on a logarithmic scale. In other words, the two servers shared half the food, the next pair split a quarter, and so on until leaving a slither of the food each of the poor first years. Sometimes you could score some custard skin. The teachers would walk around, obviously peeved at even having to be there, yet oblivious to the injustice that was taking place right under their eyes.

The three ice cream vans outside the school gate benefited directly from the fact that the lower school kids were emerging from the lunch hall, still hungry. Each ice cream man had merit. Wrench's van was decrepit but he sold real, old-fashioned ice cream. Wrench was an ugly old man. It was not just physical, unwashed ugliness, his mean-spiritedness matched his appearance. However, his scoops of ice cream were heavenly. My friend Darren Trainor, called it 'Nectar of the Gods.' Of course, thinking his superior product could 'sell itself' was Wrench's downfall. The quality over quantity philosophy was not particularly embraced by adolescents.

Mr. Softie was far more generous and his swirling yellow ice cream, albeit machine-generated, was tasty enough and more filling than

Wrench's divine nectar. He had his steady stream of regular customers, demeanour courted by his consistently cheerful. He obviously enjoyed his job.

The third van, Beano, generated taste-free, fluorescent white ice cream. It was so cheap that he could afford to balance huge swirls on top of the cone and still make a healthy profit. Wrench was persistently disgusted with Beano's 'shit.' Beano was rumoured to be involved with the Italian mafia, and he never denied the accusations. He was a headstrong Sicilian, who spoke with a stereotypical comical Italian accent.

"You no lika ma ica creama, Meesta Wrench? Fangola! Whicha means fooka offa!" he shouted, when he saw Wrench glaring at one of his mega-cones.

"Shit, pure unadulterated shit!" Wrench shouted back.

"I tella you what is shit. You is shit!" Beano retorted.

Beano had no boundaries nor fear. He would let kids sit in his van and tell them dirty stories about girls. This offended Mr Softie, who saw himself as providing a service and considered himself a role model - an ambassador for the ice cream industry.

And so, the famous ice cream wars of 1966 begun. Firstly, Wrench and Mr. Softy got together and decided that they needed to get rid of Beano. They formed a pact, where they would temporarily take a cut in profits to price Beano out of the market.

I came out of lunch one Tuesday morning to witness a huge queue at Wrench's van. Sure enough, Wrench was giving sixpenny double ninety-nines. Double scoops and two flakes all for a silver sixpence. Mr. Softy, who made very few sales that day, consoled himself with the fact that Beano made even less. As Wrench drove off he made the mistake of giving the thumbs up to Mr. Softy, followed by the V-sign to Beano. This alerted Beano to the pact and the second stage of the battle was hatched.

The next day Mr Softy brought cans of mixed fruit and his cones included heaps of ice cream, 2 chocolate flakes and a ladle of bits of peaches, cherries, grapes and pears. Wrench also continued his double 99 deal. Beano was livid.

The final day of the Ice Cream Wars went from sublime to ridiculous. Wrench halved the price of his double 99, quickly followed by a matching drop by Mr. Softy. Where there would previously be twenty boys hanging around the vans there was suddenly a couple of hundred, all clutching threepenny bits.

This was when Beano lost it.

"Okay Free ice cream," Beano declared. Instantly the queues diverted to Beano's. Moreover, he was handing out free cigarettes to any pupil that wanted one. Kids were in his van, playing the radio at full blast. Mr. Softy was horrified at the awful role-modelling to which they were being subjected. Mr. Wrench was possessed by a different sentiment. Suddenly, Wrench was standing outside Beano's van, clutching a tire lever.

"Sod off, Beano!" yelled Wrench, bright red with anger.

"Fangola!" Beano replied.

I'd heard about the legendary fights that happened at high school but I was not expecting my first experience to involve ice cream men.

Wrench bashed a serious dent in Beano's front wing with his tyre lever. The crowd gasped and began to chant, "Beano, Beano, Beano!"

"You bloody little wop! You're a dead man!" shouted Wrench. His eyes were glazed over and he would have been able to genuinely claim 'temporary insanity' at any murder trial.

Beano would have been well-advised to have driven off but instead he leapt over the counter and fearlessly marched up to the blunt-instrument clutching, semi-psychotic, Wrench and stood less than a foot away.

"You don'ta know whatta you're dealing with, Meesta Wrench! We will kill you and your family," Beano retorted.

The chanting was replaced by pin-drop silence. Any doubts about Beano's mafia connections were instantly dissipated. This was not a school yard scrap. This was two fully-fledged adults threatening to end each other's lives. I suddenly felt nauseous and was having trouble keeping-down my triple-flaked fruit-laden wafer. I noticed that many of my peers were turning as pale as me.

Wrench began to tremble almost to the point of convulsion, then he said, "I don't have any family." He turned and climbed into his van and drove off.

Beano turned to the crowd, looking like he expected applause. But it had become too serious and the silence hung in the air. Then he walked back to his van, and shouted, "Getta outta ma vanna!" The boys scampered out, without needing to be told twice. Beano jumped in the vacated driver's seat and sped off, without even securing the cones, flakes or syrups, which flew out of the serving window.

Mr. Softy had a sudden monopoly. He attributed this change in fortune to his positive role modelling. Beano never returned and it took Wrench three weeks to creep back. I had a different set of sentiments toward Wrench because he had shown bravery in tackling the crazy Italian and possibly the mafia. However, my bigger thought was that he had no family: no parents; no siblings; no wife; no children. Nobody to care about or to be bothered whether he lived or died, including himself. Ice cream was not just his job, it was his entire raison d'etre. In a world where synthetics were cheap skating children just to increase profits, Wrench had chosen to adhere to the old-fashioned product and he was willing to defend it to the grave.

78

Chapter 7: Teachers

There were three controlling mechanisms at Hartley High School: Impositions, detentions and the dreaded corporal punishment.

An imposition, or 'impo' consisted of a 3-paragraph essay, chosen for its boringness, to the point of being soul-destroying. It started thus: "When an individual is miserable, what does it most of all behove him to do? To complain of this man or of that, of this thing or of that? Not so at all. But the reverse of so................." Even the minor offenders in the school, such as myself, soon learned to write paragraph one, ad verbatim, and did not even need the original to copy. Impositions could be given by teachers or prefects and those who foolishly tried to manipulate their way out of an impo soon found their name added to the detention list.

Detention meant remaining behind for an hour on a Friday, and copying out an imposition. Although it only added an hour of school-time, the added burden of missing the school bus and having to catch a Hartley then Sutton Green bus would make it so that it was after six o'clock when you got home. Furthermore, the bus contract was only valid on school buses, unless it stated via Hartley, and so quite often bus fare was required. On a detention evening, you might have to forfeit dinner money and ice cream money just to pay for the journey. Assuming that your morning had been organized enough to incorporate breakfast, this meant a possible ten hours between two Weetabix and the evening meal, if your mum was patient enough to have saved you some food.

The slipper or the cane was the ultimate deterrent. Some teachers just used it when necessary, like Ernie Ball, my brother's home room teacher gave me three swipes with his slipper, for writing 'Jimi Hendrix' on the homework timetable on his notice board. It was two for the offence and one for not managing to touch my toes on command. My first high school slippering didn't hurt much and my pride far outweighed the pain.

"Thank you, sir," I told Ernie, as was the tradition and he acknowledged this with a no-hard-feelings nod. An enhanced mutual respect emerged from the encounter. However, some teachers were downright sadistic.

Mr. Hardman, the history teacher once sketched on the board a large triangle, to represent England, with a small triangle to the west, which was obviously Ireland. He seemed to be in a jocular mood and even popped a tiny triangle between the two and asked what that represented.

I raised my hand and as he nodded for me to reply. "The Isle of Man, sir," I blurted out.

"Excellent Wells," he responded, obviously remembering my name because he had previously taught my elder brother.

"I went there this summer………..," I started to explain, but he cut me off mid-sentence.

"I want you all to draw a map of Great Britain," he said, "and label the main Roman roads," He added Watling Street to his triangular England, as an example. "But don't just draw triangles, I want a proper England and Ireland."

He gave out atlases to help. I diligently sketched England and Ireland, still feeling a little pride that I had impressed the teacher with my knowledge of the place that I had spent my summer vacation, some weeks earlier. My Cornwall was a little elongated and my Scotland was somewhat slimmer than reality but he had not really emphasized the importance of accuracy. Some years earlier I had a plastic outline of the United Kingdom as a birthday present and I had drawn around the shape hundreds of times.

While most teachers felt that predictability was their strongest weapon, Hardman enjoyed his reputation of being unpredictable. As he walked up and down the aisles, he spontaneously kicked Toftie's football, so hard it bounced off three walls and knocked a complete set of textbooks onto the floor. His attitude seemed to be, *"This is my classroom and I'll do whatever I damned well please."* To First Years this was terrifying. In Junior school, the teachers had known that even when they were acting in *loco parentis* they were still accountable to parents. However, high school teachers had full discretion. They could bully individuals or even a whole class on a whim without repercussions.

Hardman stopped at Fatty Witherspoon's desk and picked up his work and in a supercilious voice asked, "So England's triangular now is it, Mr Witherspoon?"

"Don't know, sir," cowered Fatty Witherspoon.

"Who else has drawn a triangle?" he asked, sustaining his creamy tones. Barry Adams hand went up. "Well at least you're honest Adams," he added, turning his glare toward Lawson Whittle.

"Whittle?" he asked, raising an eyebrow. Whittle reluctantly raised his hand, since it was now apparent that the teacher had already noticed his mistake.

"S-s-sorry, sir," Whittle stammered.

"Why don't you three stooges come out to the front of the class," he smiled. The class snickered, anticipating that the teacher was about to have a bit of fun at their expense. Especially when Hardman made us all compress our desks to the back of the room, leaving a large empty space for a skit at the front.

There was a buzz of excitement around the room, and Adams was still grinning as Hardman asked him to face the wall and touch his toes. However, the class collectively held their breath as Hardman produced a ⅜ inch bamboo cane from behind his desk and accelerated across the room to gain maximum impetus, as the whipping sound was followed by the yelping sound of the unsuspecting Adams.

"Sit down Adams," he told the boy, "you only get one because you were honest.

It seemed unfair because Witherspoon, who already had anticipatory tears flowing, had not really lied either. But he was bent over and subject to three similar strokes. I really felt for Fatty Witherspoon because it could have been any of us. The teacher had not over-stressed the importance of not drawing triangles and I winced as each stroke hit Witherspoon's bottom.

Whittle had to be admired because his face never showed a glimmer of emotion as he touched his toes on command. Nor did he cry, as the cane shattered into pieces on his backside. The Gods appeared to be on his side because he only ended up getting one lash. Also, he was chosen to return the broken cane and the Corporal Punishment (CP) log to the school office. This gave him an opportunity to lick his wounds in private, without further humiliation.

In hindsight, Hardman was just looking for an excuse to set an example that day. He already had the cane and CP log in advance and he just wanted to 'set the tone' for the year. I hated him for what he did to Fatty Witherspoon. When we left the room, I noticed that lines of blood were seeping through his trousers. It was obvious that his bottom would be scarred for weeks and his mind would be scarred for life. Witherspoon was absent as often as he was present for the rest of the term. And each time he did turn up he was noticeably larger.

More sadistic than Hardman was the PE teacher, Simeon Westwood. He had been a footballer for Port Vale, and then moved into the teaching profession, as he had started to age. Westwood could not let anything pass. While other teachers drank tea during their break time, Fizzer Westwood, would find dastardly ways to creep up on smoker's corner. Each time he would grab a hand full of smokers and march them down to the deputy headmaster's office for a caning.

"I wasn't smoking, sir," was the standard claim and sometimes an innocent would get corralled by mistake.

"Fizzing heck, son," he would exclaim, hence his nickname, "do you think I'm stupid?"

"No sir," was the only viable response to that question. Most teachers accepted that if kids wanted to smoke there was no way to stop them. It was better to know where they smoked, and turn a blind eye to it. Also, preventing them smoking only made them crotchety in class. And after all, most teachers smoked. Most teachers would probably have answered "Yes" to Fizzer's 'Do you think I'm stupid?' question. However, Westwood saw himself as the school police, whether it was smoking, fighting, minor school uniform infractions or avoiding showers after PE, Fizzer was there to enforce the law. He even had Toby Brown caned for farting, or "contaminating the atmosphere," as it was reported in the CP log. In Fizzer's defence, we were all gagging at the 'contamination,' deliberate or not.

"At least he's not picking on a Mongol," I thought, seven years on from seeing Johnny Marston's 'smack bottom' in the nursery, for a similar offense.

One day we entered the gym to see that Fizzer had set out rubber mats, each with two pairs of boxing gloves. We were given very little direction, just 'choose a partner, a mat, and put on the gloves.' I ended up with Toby Brown, more by default than choice. I decided to keep my punches aimed at the face, not wanting to risk any inadvertent gas releases.

"Go!" said Fizzer, blowing his whistle to officially start proceedings, without further direction. Luckily, my dad had given Andrew and I a few coaching sessions about boxing and the instincts came straight back to me. I knew to guard my face with the gloves and use momentum to maximize my punching power. Sure enough, it was easy to pick off a few pokes to Toby's face and the parrying of his counter punches was effortless. It was fun for a while, until I looked over and saw my friend, Darren Trainor having seven shades of shit knocked out of him, by an overzealous David Waterhouse. Trainor was on the verge of tears.

"Wanna swap?" I shouted.

"Are we allowed?" he answered.

"I think so," I answered. And so, I moved to Waterhouse's mat and Trainor took on Brown. Trainor and Brown liked the arrangement, as their mutual cowardice turned it into a tic-tac-toe scenario. Unfortunately, Waterhouse relished the opportunity of a more challenging opponent. He came at me with both guns blazing. Waterhouse was freakishly strong for a small stocky kid and his shorter height seemed an advantage, as he could get in easily with uppercuts to my chin. All I could do was punch down on the top of his head. What had started as a fun lesson had evolved into a nightmare and whatsmore he had boundless energy, whereas I was totally depleted. Waterhouse caught me with a couple of hits that made me reel. Fizzer was the Rulemeister, under most circumstances, but he had decided to experiment with an innovative approach at the most inopportune time. His normal controlling self would have you shivering impatiently, as he over-explained, but on this day, he had chosen to try some *Avant Garde* student-led strategy.

"Good Waterhouse!" Fizzer exclaimed, as he watched me tottering on the edge of the mat. Then I had an idea that I should have had 3 minutes earlier. I stepped off the mat.

"You're fizzing disqualified Wells," came the welcome fizz of Fizzer. Waterhouse tutted but felt he had to obey the rule. Suddenly, there were kids stepping off the mats all over the whole gym, as I had inadvertently shown the exit route from their own misery. Surprisingly, in many cases both members of the pair stepped off together. Waterhouse and I sat down on the mat, and soon the other pairs followed suit.

"So, what have we learned?" asked Fizzer

"We need rules, sir," smarmed Whittle

"Very good, Whittle," Fizzer replied, "and what happens if there are no rules?"

Everyone remained quiet, some afraid to say the wrong thing, others still dazed by their ordeals. Fizzer looked around and I made the fatal mistake of making eye contact, triggering him to say, "Wells?"

"Yes, Sir," I replied

"Do you know what anarchy is?"

"No Sir," I replied.

"Anarchy is what happens when there are no rules," Fizzer stated, "you have just experienced anarchy. I want you to all think about that."

"A powerful lesson," I contemplated.

Then Whittle, who had an apparent death wish raised his hand.

"What is it Whittle?" Fizzer asked, obviously vexed that he had just rounded off a life lesson and now this brainless urchin was going to ruin the moment.

"But sir, we made up our own rules. We all decided that we had to keep fighting till somebody won and that we could not step off the mat. So that was two rules."

"So, what's your point, Whittle?" said Fizzer rolling his eyes.

"That people don't always need somebody controlling them with rules, sir." Whittle pontificated, "People will regulate themselves if they are left to work things out between them, sir."

"You're a fizzing idiot, boy!" Fizzer retorted, "Hit the showers everybody!"

It was amazing that this lesson in thuggery had somehow turned into a lesson in philosophy. It was brilliant that Fizzer Westwood had contrived to use boxing to educate us in the need for rules. It was even more stunning that Whittle had chosen the same example to illustrate to the domineering gym teacher that his overbearing ways were not always necessary. The shame lay in the fact that the teacher was too opinionated to hear the wisdom in the words of his pupil.

In total contrast, Hovis Brown, the music teacher could not have cared less about the learning or behaviour of any of his students. Every lower school class visited Hovis for a single period a week. He saw every first, second and third year but he was almost oblivious to their existence. Basically, textbooks were given out at the start of class and collected at the end, whilst the teacher entertained himself playing his grand piano.

The textbooks had illustrated stories about composers and we all spent the whole lesson adding to the illustrations. Most of the pictures had genitals added to the people but more entertaining were the speech bubbles. Of course, most were just vulgar comments, laced heavily with the F-word, but others had some clever additions. For instance, someone had drawn a pile of poo behind Beethoven's piano bench and labelled it, 'Beethoven's Last Movement.' Someone else wrote, 'a stool on a stool.' A chapter on Vivaldi's four seasons, had "Don't forget Frankie Valet!" Another wag had cleverly taken the William Tell story and edited in pictures of the Lone Ranger and Tonto because they used the same theme music.

There was only one lesson that Hovis even interacted with the students and that was the week when we were auditioning for the choir. Basically, students were expected to stand up, alphabetically, and sing, "Strangers in the Night," by Frank Sinatra.

Now, being a Wells, I had quite a while to mentally rehearse. In my mind, Frank Sinatra sang in a deep voice but Adams was given a full flourishing introduction before launching into a soprano rendition, "Strangers in the night, exchanging glances, wondering in the night, what were the chances, we'd be making love before the night was through," he sang.

"Good effort, son," Hovis told him, diplomatically gesturing for him to sit down. Bamford and Bolton got the same flamboyant piano introduction and eight bars of song to impress. Both failed.

Then the most beautiful woman's voice emerged from the shy lips of Chadwick and he became the first inductee into the Hartley High School choir.

"Magnificent!" exclaimed Hovis, as a real teardrop rolled down his cheek, much to our entertainment. The next few kids butchered the song, maybe because they had felt intimidated. Hovis gradually reduced his four-bar introduction to a single note, purely to give the key.

Gotham and Trainor did enough to get a "You'll do," from the music teacher but then there was a stream of four boys who decimated the song and Hovis seemed to lose interest in even giving the first note. We were all awaiting Timpson's effort because he was the unofficial class clown and we were not to be disappointed.

"Okay Timpson, let's hear what you can do to Sinatra's masterpiece." he said, rolling his eyes in anticipation. Little did he realize that he had just delivered the greatest set up of all time.

A glint came in Timpson's eye and he begun to click his fingers with a beat that really did not fit with Strangers in the Night, and he launched into his song, "You keep saying, you've got something for me," he sang, as the whole class erupted in hysterics, "something you call love I must confess." Hovis looked perplexed as to what was happening. He was the only person in the room that did not know that Frank's daughter, Nancy Sinatra had also sung a masterpiece. "These boots were made for walkin', and that's just what they'll do. One of these days these boots are gonna walk all over you!"

"Sit down, Timpson," said Hovis Brown, confirming just what a truly out-of-touch teacher he was.

Tattersfield stood up and said, "You missed me out, sir."

"Good," responded Hovis, without really concentrating. It was unfortunate because Tattersfield was victimized by every student in the place. Even non-bullies would make exceptions for Tattersfield. Even though the music teacher had his mind on something else when he dismissed Tattersfield, the boy sat down again, with another notch in his persecution complex.

By the time, Hovis got to the W's his disinterest was flaunting itself.

"Wells," Hovis said

I stood up, took a deep breath and started, "Strangers in th…"

"Next," interrupted the Music teacher.

I turned to my friend, Darren Trainor, and said, "Well that was pretty painless.

"Don't you believe it," he joked, feigning to put his fingers in his ears. Then he quickly changed the subject, "What about Sinatra's masterpiece, "These boots were made for walking. It was brill."

"Brill," I agreed. My entire singing career had consisted of two and a half words.

Twee was my favourite teacher. It was unfortunate that he had chosen to teach the one science discipline that he could not pronounce, Chemistwee.

"Everweebody take out your Chemistwee books," he directed.

"Twee, twee, twee," impersonators all around the room echoed. It was an involuntary response for some of my classmates. I felt a little sorry for Twee and I half-wished he'd turn 'Hardman' on them. However, he was far too nice to resort to the cane. Instead, he had an ignore-it-and-it-will-go-away philosophy. It never went away.

The thing that I liked about Twee was his willingness to let us do all the experiments, from which the more experienced teachers shied away.

"This expewement is simple: Mix Sulfuwic Acid with marble chips in a conical flask." He demonstrated as he went. "Insert a wubber bung with a deliverwee tube."

"Wubber bung, wubber bung,' Darren Trainor whispered in my ear.

"Bubble hydwogen from the deliverwee tube through some soap solution," Twee demonstrated.

We all marvelled as little bubbles arose from the end of the tube and floated gracefully from the surface of the soap solution.

"Wubber bung, wubber bung," Trainor continued to whisper, which caused us both to snicker.

Twee turned around and decided to refocus me, by firing a question, "Wells, why are the bubbles floating?"

I was lucky because I had learned the answer in my physics class. "Because hydrogen is lighter than air, sir."

"Excellent, Wells," he responded, reminding me why I considered him my favourite teacher. He then turned his attention to my friend. "Tell me Trainor, why isn't the hydrogen making the flask float?"

Without hesitation Trainor replied, "Because of the weight of the flask, sir."

"Good, Trainor," said Twee.

"And the weight of the wubber bung, sir" added Trainor, much to the hilarity of the class. Twee did not react. I wondered whether maybe the pronunciation sounded correct to him, so he did not even notice.

"Phase thwee is to pop the bubble with a lighted splint," the teacher explained. "Now make sure that the bubble has completely left the appawatus before you light it. I will wepeat that, don't light the bubble till it is floating fweely."

It was the best experiment ever. Boys were chasing soap bubbles of hydrogen all around the room lancing them with burning sticks. It was hard to explain the ecstatic sensation as the skewered bubble magically popped into a yellow flame. It was at that point that I decided I wanted to be a chemist, when I grew up. Unfortunately, that aspiration only lasted about two minutes.

Chemistry and impetuosity are not good bedfellows. Somewhere in the back of my mind I knew that there was a reason to wait until the bubble was clear of the soap.

"Boom!" the flask took off like a rocket. Who knows how far it would have gone if the chemistry lab ceiling had not been in the way. It all happened in a flash but, like most accidents, the shock made it feel like it was in slow motion. Unfortunately, there was not enough time to appreciate the launch before the flask, containing sulfuric acid, was plummeting back down to earth.

"Crash!" the flask hit the table, as we cowered trying to cover our faces with our hands. I fully expected to feel the rush of glass shards and the sting of acid in my face. However, by some miracle, the flask remained intact.

"Don't panic!" yelled Twee, openly panicking. Once he had established that we were all unharmed he turned to me and said, "That was weally, weally stupid, Wells!"

I could not argue against that. I also had a newfound respect for Hydrogen.

Pedro Rouse, was my rotund French teacher, who was actually Spanish. He was one of those people who had a permanent seven o'clock shadow, rather like the cartoon character, Fred Flintstone. He had been selected to pioneer a new language learning style with my class. Apparently, English schools were churning out students who could write French but were an embarrassment, when they came to speak it.

Pedro would always start the class with a description of the French culture. For instance, he told us that, Frenchmen kissed one another on each cheek when they first greeted.

"All four of them," Trainor whispered in my ear, causing me to giggle.

Pedro assumed that my laughter was about the men kissing and he felt obliged to explain, "It's not a romantic thing, it's only like people shaking hands." Then he added, "Of course, they never do that in Spain."

Another day, he gave an interesting example of the cultural differences saying, "If a Frenchman is on a train, eating his sandwiches, he is expected to offer food to everyone in the compartment. However, it was also tradition that everyone has to politely decline." It seemed nonsensical but then I recalled the Isle of Man trip and wondered whether I was supposed to have rejected Barry Wise's Kit-Kat and John Trotter's Cheese and Branston Pickle sandwich. At the time, I felt like it would have been downright anti-social to refuse them.

Our French class had been selected for an experimental approach, called, "Ecouter, Regardez, Repetez." Which meant, "Listen, look, repeat," And that was our job for the entire year. The film strip was set up and a picture of Janine, washing her face was projected on the wall.

Rouse switched on the tape recorder, which would announce, "Janine fais sa toilette."

We all droned "Janine fais sa toilette" Apparently, it literally meant that Janine does her toileting, which really meant 'washes her face.'

The tape repeated it and so did we. Then the tape went, "Ping" signalling that it was time to turn to the next slide.

The whole class went "Ping!" too.

"Janine brossez ca cheveau," was the full emersion dialogue for the picture of Janine brushing her hair.

"I'm falling in love with Janine," Darren Trainor whispered in my ear. Causing me to laugh, which caused Rouse to clip me across the back of the head. Trainor was always getting me clobbered.

"Monsieur Wells, quelle passé?" he asked. I think he was asking what was so funny.

"It's Trainor, sir" I started to say.

"En francais, en francais," Rouse insisted, meaning that I should say it in French. He even switched off the tape, giving me time to think out my answer. He had obviously chosen this moment to make an example. I was just hoping that he was not going to go 'Hardman' on me.

"Darreen," I said,

"Oui?" the French teacher urged.

"Darreen aime Janine," I said.

Trainor blushed and Pedro cracked up, which signalled permission for the whole class to relax and have a laugh.

Then Pedro turned to Darren Trainor and asked, "C'est vrai?" meaning 'is this true? 'And we all leaned forward on our chairs, waiting to see if he said, "Oui," or "No." The atmosphere was such that either response would have been humorous.

Trainor milked the moment, like the undiscovered comic genius that he was, then he took a deep breath and went, "Ping."

Uproar ensued. Even Pedro Rouse saw the hilarity.

Chapter 8: Top Ranking.

My transition from junior to senior school gave me the opportunity to implement an image change. Hardly anybody at Hartley High knew me, so they did not know about my painful shyness with girls. They also did not know that girls had enjoyed making me blush mercilessly throughout my Junior school days. Now I was I high-schooler, I could talk boldly about my interest in girls without fear of having to put my money where my mouth was, so to speak.

The Top Rank was a new nightclub, that realized that there was a whole market of teenagers, wanting to go to a disco on a Saturday afternoon. It was not much different than their elder night-time counterparts, except that ice slushies were sold for a greater profit than the evening alcohol and the teens were less trouble. All they wanted to do was show off their mod clothes, dance, flirt, and snog up corners. A couple of DJ's took it in turns to dance on the stage whilst they played the latest records, occasionally throwing in the odd prize-winning game and playing requests and dedications. Girls would dance in groups around their handbags, so that their hands were free for demonstrative dancing and their bags remained safely in sight.

Boys could dance nearby the girls and close in if any magnetism occurred. Or they could move painlessly on without suffering the full force of rejection. I was glad of the training I had at the Isle of Man because I felt reasonably comfortable on the dancefloor. A top rank tradition was that everybody got up to dance to a tune called "March of the Mods." Basically, everybody marched in an anticlockwise direction, four taps with the right foot; four taps with the left; two-footed hop forward; two-footed hop back; walk three steps forward. It took little mastery and it had all the elements of an old-fashioned barn-dance.

For some inexplicable reason, a Greek tune called Zorba's Dance always followed, which was a communal sideways dance that started slow and gathered pace, leaving everyone exhilarated and exhausted.

I was just about to rest after Zorba's dance and a girl came up to me and said, "Will you go out with my friend?"

She pointed over to a group of three girls, two with long blonde hair seemed oblivious but the third, with short brown hair, kept shifting from foot to foot and glancing sideways.

"Yeah," I said, trying to be cool but dying a thousand deaths inside. Her friend nodded to her but then nobody knew the next move. So, the friend, who was also quite nice, grabbed my hand and pulled me across the room to formalize the introduction.

"This is Carol," she told me. I nodded politely.

"This is…...this is……. this is the bit where you say your name," said the ever-more appealing friend.

"This is…." she tried again.

"Oh…. Martin," I replied.

"O'Martin, he must be Irish," said the waggish girl, playing cupid. She grabbed Carol's hand and linked it to my own, and before we knew it we were in a Snoggers' Alcove, practicing kissing on each other. I was remembering the rules of engagement - lips slightly apart, lightly moistened, slow movements, no clash of noses. It seemed to be going quite well, when all of a sudden, Hold Tight, by Dave Dee, Dozy, Beaky, Mick and Titch, started up.

"Oh, I love this song," said Carol, dragging me onto the dance floor. The dance was a little awkward because it was hard to know where to look. When the song ended, I was left standing alone, as Carol rushed to report back to her giggling friends. It took me a few minutes to realize that I was no longer 'going out' with Carol. I felt a little used but it was okay because I was already wondering about how to break up with her, anyway.

The Top Wank, as we sometimes called it in tribute to my Chemistry teacher, was my new favourite place. The music was superb: they only played groovy bands like The Who, Move, Hollies and Kinks, and none of the radio-dross like The Seekers, Tom Jones and Val Doonican.

I got a pair of groovy trousers called 'hipsters, 'which were not comfortable because the belt was low on the hips and it was a bugger to try and keep your shirt tucked in. I also bought a new mod shirt each week; I became that Dedicated Follower of Fashion that The Kinks had been singing about. My image change was complete, and I became a regular up Snoggers' Corner.

One Saturday, The Wank, to which we had further reduced it, was invaded by the entire Trotter entourage. I had not seen them since the Isle of Man, and I was excited to see them, but many people feared their reputation. It occurred to me that I had not really revealed my relationship with the legendary family to my friends or my brother. So, when Kenny and his disciples approached me, Andrew looked perturbed. Notorious thugs were making a bee-line toward his brother.

"Please tell me you haven't snogged his bloody sister," Andrew whispered, without moving his lips.

Ken Trotter stood squarely in front of me.

"Told you it was him," came John Trotter's voice from behind.

"What's up Kenny, you got something hard in your trousers you want me to squeeze?" I asked, remembering the knife incident.

I heard my brother grimace, like he thought I'd just signed my own death warrant. Trotter waited a couple of awkward seconds and then burst into laughter.

"Bloody hilarious,' he laughed, offering a handshake.

"Nice hipsters, Martin," said John, also shaking my hand. Of course, Barry Wise, who now had his hair back-combed, followed suit and Sonia gave me a massive hug. Andrew and all my friend's jaws dropped.

"Is Sammy here?" I asked Sonia, the DJ's booming voice gave the answer.

"I have a request from a girl called Sammy, this number is especially for Martin. Sammy says, 'Remember the Isle of Man?' It's The Move and they're about to call the Fire Brigade.

"Cast your mind back......." started Roy Wood. Instantly my mind was cast back, to that concert in Douglas, and we all began to dance. Sammy raced from the stage and flung her arms around me like I was a long-lost friend. I suddenly felt like the cat that got the cream and my esteem climbed to new heights.

At the end of the song the DJ announced that they were going to hold a competition for

Junior Disc Jockey of the Week. They needed six people on stage, three boys and three girls. Without thinking, I let people whisk me onto the stage. The DJ asked us all our names and then we all had to dance while a song called The Hunter gets Captured by the Game, played out. I'd never heard the song before and it had a funky rhythm that was hard to dance to. However, when they asked the audience to vote at the end of the song, I got the biggest cheer. They hung a miniature disco ball, on a chain around my neck and I was the DJ for the next 30 minutes. I announced each record as it came up and then danced uninhibitedly. I even had a girl come up and ask for my autograph but I was not sure whether she was taking the piss or not. I signed anyway.

My final act as Junior DJ of the Week was to announce, "I'd like to dedicate this song to Sammy Jeffries, it's The Troggs, 'A girl like you.'"

Sammy curtseyed and blew me a kiss, which I thought was altogether classy. My affiliation with the Trotter brigade was helping affect my image change and becoming a defining moment.

Chapter 9: Secrets

Mum was usually an open book. However, she finally got on a nursing course and it seemed to raise her self-worth and self-confidence. She met a whole new network of friends and started to get a little shirtier with my dad.

Previous household chores that they had both taken for granted as mum's job were suddenly being reassessed. All of a sudden, there was 'no reason why dad couldn't run a duster round.' Previously, she had kept her criticisms to his inability to do masculine jobs, such as knocking a nail in a wall, or whitewashing the outhouse. However, now he was also being held accountable for washing the dishes, feeding Doodle, putting the empty milk bottles on the step, and many more tasks that we were not aware existed. Apparently, it was useless paying Fred the Window Cleaner for his efforts on the outside windows if nobody took care of the insides. In his defines, dad took her point and tried to step up his game but she saw his cooperation as passive aggressive.

I was not sure whether his compliance was genuine or perverted. One day, he made the mistake of trying to surprise her by washing all the net curtains in the house. He got them down just fine and the filthy water draining from the washing machine proved that the curtains had benefited. However, for some reason, dad waited for mum's return, before putting them back in the window. Perhaps he wanted to be certain that she knew that he had washed them. He seemed genuinely surprised that he did not earn any kudos.

"What have you done that for?" she demanded

"I was just trying to help, dear," dad responded

"Help, my arse!" she retorted, "Trying to make me look like an unfit wife with dirty curtains, more like!"

"Don't be daft," he responded. "You know Ted and Bertha are coming tonight?" Ted and Bertha were their life-long friends. They found the banter between mum and dad to be a constant source of amusement.

"The whole bloody world will know they're here because I'm not putting the bloody curtains back up, tonight!"

Sure enough, Ted and Bertha arrived and immediately the conversation got around to my dad's new duties.

"Looks different in here, Pete. Have you painted since we came last, mate?" Ted asked.

"Heaven forbid," mum muttered, unable to contain her contempt.

"Well it seems a bit brighter in here," said Ted, pretending to be oblivious to the undercurrents.

"He's right Bet, Bertha chipped in, it does seem different."

"Well his majesty here, is having a few problems adjusting to our new job-sharing regime, now I'm working full-time," Mum explained.

"I'm pulling my weight," dad spurted out, indignantly.

"He's pulling something," mum declared, causing Bertha to nearly spit out her Babycham.

"So, what's he done, this time?" joked Ted, trying to lighten the mood but sustain the entertainment.

"What's he done?" mum mimicked, "tell 'em what you've done Mr Muck!"

"Ha, Mr Muck!" Ted echoed.

"I washed the net curtains." dad explained, looking for sympathy.

"Bastard!" said Bertha.

"I know," said mum.

"I don't get it" said the perplexed Ted.

"That's what I said," dad concurred.

"Well........," started mum.

"I've got this one, Beryl," Bertha took over, "if he had wanted to help........"

"Course he did," Ted defended.

"If he'd genuinely wanted to help," Bertha continued, "he could have saved her a job, not made her an extra one. He could have mopped the kitchen floor, vacuumed the living room, got the cobwebs down, cleaned the toilet. Am I right Bet, am I right."

Mum was furiously nodding. It was nice to have someone deliver her resentments, almost therapeutic.

"But worse than not helping," the rant continued, "he found something that made it look like she was a negligent housewife."

She turned to mum and assured her, "Everybody knows that's not true, Bet."

Then she turned to dad and said, "Peter, you think you're being a smartarse but net curtains are the easiest target of all. You could go to anybody's house in this road and wash a load of shit out of their net curtains. That's what net curtains are for, Pete. To gather shit!"

She turned to me and apologized, "Sorry kids." We were desperately trying not to snicker.

Then, she addressed the whole group, "Right, everybody put your coats on, Ted's taking us out to the Bernie Inn, to celebrate Beryl becoming a nurse."

Ted was agog. Her rant was under the guise of advocating for Beryl but Ted knew that he was the true inspiration for the venom. It was loaded with subliminal digs at Ted. Not least of all, her husband was notoriously tight with his money, which was a source of embarrassment for Bertha. So, when she committed him to footing the bill at an expensive restaurant, Bernie Inn, he knew that the worm also had turned on him.

"Tell you one thing I'm never doing," Ted whispered in dad's ear.

"What's that?" dad asked.

"Washing net curtains, ha ha," he quipped.

Mum had a plastic memo book, dedicated entirely to recording her work shifts. She would work a couple of weeks alternating between early and late shifts. So, some days, dad would pick her up, as late as midnight, if there had been a last-minute emergency, like a death. Then he would be dropping her off again at 7:00am the next morning. On top of that, each month she had to work a whole week of nights. She never complained about the trainee nurses' outrageous workload because she was just glad to be back on her career track. She had initially wanted to be a nurse, but love marriage and babies, not necessarily in that order, had hijacked that particular dream. Mum's life was like a steeplechase race, with regular hurdles that she took in her stride and the occasional obstacle that side-tracked her progress.

She rarely got a full weekend off, which dad hated but mum loved. It gave her time to herself, as well as transferring some weekend chores to dad.

One day, I peeked in her diary to check her following week's shifts and I was intrigued by something she had written; there was a letter B by Tuesday, her next day off. At first the mysterious B simply puzzled me but then it began to eat away at the inquisitive region of my brain. Then, when we got home from school on that Tuesday, mum was in a mood that could only be described as euphoric. Whatever B was, it had worked wonders for her mood.

I snooped in her diary for further clues and, once again a B had appeared for the following Monday, another day off. Furthermore, I arrived home from school to another uncharacteristically cheerful mum.

This time she was singing to herself, "They say we look pretty good together." It was not even a dross song, it was Substitute by The Who. It was like she was ten years younger. The third week, mum came home from work, the day before her next arranged B-day. She had a last-minute shift change and she was going to have to switch her day off. I watched her go to her diary to alter the shift, and a look of panic came over her face. Next thing I knew, she was using a knife to tease four penny coins from the family piggy bank, donning her coat and heading off to the phone box.

The mystery was beyond intrigue, it was worrying. Mum obviously had a secret rendezvous planned each time she had free time.

"Where did you go?" I asked her, when she returned from the phone call.

"Oh, I needed to go and get some bacon for your dad's dinner," she told me.

It did not add up. Part of me needed to know what was going on and another part was scared to know. She was showing more and more signs of discontent with dad, which I had attributed to her newfound empowerment. However, that would not explain why she was having a secret rendezvous each week with B. She did have a new friend called Brenda but she was open about seeing her.

Later, I looked to see if she had added anything to her datebook. Sure, enough there was another addition for Wednesday. It said, "Bernie."

Now I was convinced, mum was having an affair. She was obviously meeting a man called Bernie. It was a horrible thought. How could she act so normal, when she was carrying this huge secret? Sure enough, on Wednesday evening mum was singing out loud to herself.

"It's just the bright elusive butterfly of love," she sang, in tribute to Val Doonican. Meanwhile, my poor ignorant dad read The Sentinel in front of the fire, then covered his face with it and drifted into oblivious sleep. It was a talent he had acquired over the years.

Mum even asked me, "How was school today, sweetheart?"

"Okay," I responded, really wanting to say, *"How was Bernie?"* but I managed to kerb the urge.

Instead I said, "How's work?" adding "Oh I forgot, it was your day off, wasn't it?"

"Yes," she told me, "I love my job but I had a lovely day off."

"Good," I lied. It was far from good, it was the worst thing I had ever heard. And the supercilious smile on her face was really annoying me. I had to say something but she beat me to the punch.

"I want to tell you a secret, Martin," she said, lowering her voice.

"What?" I responded. I was flattered that she was about to take me into her confidence but also scared of what she might say.

"I've been doing something every week but I don't want your dad to find out. I know he wouldn't like it. Can I trust you?" she asked.

I was speechless but I nodded. I mentally braced myself for the, *"You're going to have a new daddy,"* speech.

"I've been having driving lessons." she revealed.

"What?" I asked, momentarily not able to make sense of the words. "You've been having driving lessons?" My tone must have been packed with incredulity because she seemed almost offended.

"Yes, you don't have to be a man to drive a car, you know. I've been going to Driving School every week. Bernard, my instructor, thinks I'm ready for my test but I don't want your dad to know, in case I fail," she explained.

"That's great, mum. I promise I won't tell him," I pledged.

"Good. I don't like keeping secrets from your dad," she told me, "but you know how he is?"

She was right. Two weeks later, she laid her pass certificate on the kitchen table in front of dad, as a fete accomplis.

"What's this then?" he asked.

"I've passed my driving test, dear," she explained.

Dad's mind clicked through a series of steps and implications, as he realized that his car would no longer be his alone.

"It's not all bad news, dear," she felt obliged to reassure him, having seen his mind ticking over.

"You won't have to drive me, when I work nights, or pick me up in the mornings," she explained. This was unwelcome news for dad because he would often leave us kids alone and go out to the hospital club when she was on nights. That had been our 'little secret' with dad.

It's ironic that I had had no qualms about snooping through my mum's date book because I had a huge diary that mum had pledged to never open.

"Martin, it would be a breach of trust for me to ever open your diary. Those are your private thoughts between you and yourself," she told me, deliberately whilst Andrew and Eric were in earshot. It was really a subtle moral lecture, that was meant for us all.

The diary was a planner that a medical rep had given to dad earlier in the year and he brought it home rather than discard it, as the passage of time made its existence more meaningless. When I was younger, I used to rationalize my problems with my pet hamster, Whiskey, in the shed outside. However, when Whiskey died, I took his death hard because he was my confidante. Although it sounded counter-intuitive, it was my conversations with my hamster that helped keep me sane.

With the reassurance that the diary was as safe as my hamster confessional cage, I began to rely on it to share my innermost thoughts. I could also bolster my self-confidence, knowing that modesty was not necessary.

Of my first Top Rank encounter, I wrote, "Met Carol, snogged her!" It was not detailed, it encapsulated the extent of the encounter.

On other occasions, I would write a whole story, for instance:

"The school bus conductor this morning was a dick. He would not open the door for ages, just because everyone was pushing and wouldn't line up. Then he would not let us upstairs, even though there were seats up there, and he made us stand up downstairs just to be a dick. So, I stole his spare roll of tickets."

One day in English class, Tattersfield, the school victim tapped me on the shoulder and showed me a black and white picture of a bare-breasted woman.

"Gimme that, Tattersfield!" I said, snatching it out of his hand.

"Give it back!" demanded Tattersfield, his tone already resolved to having lost it forever.

It's hard to justify why this would not count as bullying; I would not have done that to anyone else on the Planet. However, Tattersfield was one of those people who only responded to cruel jaunts. If you ever made the mistake of being nice to Tattersfield you would always regret it. He was horrible. Anyway, now I was in possession of his photo of a semi-naked woman, I had to find somewhere safe to keep it. The diary immediately sprang to mind. So, it was carefully wedged into a secret spot on a certain page of my diary. Every evening, whilst I was journaling, I would check that my diary was undisturbed from the bedside table and that the nudey pic was still firmly lodged in the deep fold of its page.

Unfortunately, one day I came home and my bedroom had been tidied. Mum was in a foul mood, which was a rare occurrence at this time. Before I could even get to my diary, she made it apparent that she knew what was in it.

"I tidied up your bedroom today," she started, "or should I say pigsty?"

"Thanks," I said, knowing that there was no satisfactory answer.

"Your book fell open on the floor, and I accidentally read what you've been up to at the Top Rank," she said.

I felt violated and shouted, "You're not supposed to read people's diaries."

"I didn't read it. I told you it fell open. But it's a good job because now I know about you 'snogging girls.' You're eleven years old for goodness sake. You're not supposed to be snogging girls."

I was horrified but the main worry was that she might have discovered my dirty picture. I mean, it was wedged in, so the chances were that it had gone unnoticed but I could hardly think straight with worry.

"I wouldn't have written it if I'd known you were going to read it," I shouted back.

"Well don't bloody do it! Then you won't be able to write about it!" she declared, without great logic. At that, she picked up my diary and flung it toward me, which is a magnanimous interpretation. Luckily, the pages did not flap apart, so there was no danger of my photo falling out. I breathed a sigh of relief but it was short-lived because, as soon as she left the room, I checked for my nude. She was gone. I checked the room but she had disappeared without a trace. Mum must have discovered it and thrown it away, which was devastating. Not because my naked woman was missing, even though I had become quite attached to her, I pretty much had every molecule of her body memorized. Most concerning, was that my mum knew more about me than I wanted her to. It was pretty devious because, where I could defend myself over her reading my diary, her silence about the picture left me totally at her mercy.

After cringing with guilt for the next month, there was one final twist to the secret saga. I was looking for somewhere to hide a packet of five Woodbine cigarettes that Jimmy Ellis had sold me for nine pence, his bus fare home. I had briefly toyed with putting them in the back of dad's top drawer in his bedroom. I pushed them right to the back but soon realized the absurdity of choosing that hiding place. So, I reached to the back of his drawer, only to discover nothing less than my naked woman. For an inexplicable reason, mum must have taken my nude and given it to dad. It made no sense, whatsoever but I took her back and placed her back in my diary. I even got some sellotape and made her a more permanent fixture.

The Wells household had become a bed of secrets. I learned that nobody could be trusted, including myself. And I only ever wrote things in my diary that I did not mind others reading. Or I would put secret symbols that only I would understand. For instance, I would draw a pair of lips if I had 'snogged' a girl, or a heart for a cuddle of any description.

Chapter 10: Bullies

Monaghan was the archetypal school bully. He was a Third Year who was picked on by everyone his own age or older and so he used to compensate by persecuting the younger students. Monaghan was detestable. The teachers and peers hated him, alike. He probably got caned more than every other pupil. It was not just his oddly flat acne-riddled face, his twisted ears or greasy blonde unkempt hair. It was more his degenerate manner. Everybody at school said dirty things about girls but the voice he used was that of a sick pervert that you would never want to go near a girl. Monaghan used to brag that he used to masturbate his Staffordshire Bull terrier, which even the most disgusting of us found disgusting.

One lunch time a rumour went around the school canteen that there was going to be a fight between Monaghan and Carl Jenkinson, who was a bit of an unknown quantity. Jenkinson was the same age as Monaghan but he had missed most of the school year. He was a quiet kid with a charming smile - the antithesis of Monaghan, who had been spreading rumours that Jenkinson had been away at Borstal, reform school for wayward children. I suspected that the gossip might have been true but Monaghan, like Tattersfield, was not allowed the same gossiping rights as other kids.

We were anticipating quite a maul, as the contestants marched to the traditional fight spot behind the gym. There were about thirty lower school spectators, hoping to see the enigmatic Jenkinson spill the blood of the detestable Monaghan. Most of us had been punched, ear-flicked or spat upon by Monaghan in the brief time that we had been at the school and watching him get his comeuppance would be a treat.

Monaghan stepped forward and motioned that he wanted to start the fight with a handshake. Jenkinson kept his arms behind his back, which made him appear extremely confident. You could see a perplexed look on Monaghan's face but this quickly turned to a dastardlier expression. Jenkinson's unguarded face was an opportunity to blindside him. Monaghan's clenched fist swung fiercely toward his opponent. If he had connected he would have knocked him out, without question. However, with the dexterity of a bullfighter, Jenkinson side-stepped the oncoming blow and I saw a flash of steel in Jenkinson's hand, bearing down on the back of Monaghan's neck. It was a fork, stolen from the canteen. The whole crowd's excitement turned to gasps of horror, as Monaghan staggered around, with a fork protruding from the back of his neck. The stabbing force had been so great that all four prongs were almost an inch deep in his neck muscles. He dropped to his knees and then the blood started to come. dark red thick blood gushed from the puncture wounds.

Monaghan looked directly in my eyes and pleaded, "Get it out, get it out!"

I looked away. In fact, everyone backed away. This was no longer the school bully that we all detested, this was the victim of a brutal crime and we were all accomplices. Then, Tattersfield, of all people, stepped forward and grabbed the fork and pulled with all his might. The blood caused his hand to slip, making the fork twist and Monaghan's face contort further. He made the sound of a pained animal.

"Bugger off, Tattersfield!" Monaghan screamed. Tattersfield was unphased by the phrase that he heard most daily.

"Hold still, you dog-wanker," responded Tattersfield, illustrating his own inability to bond socially. Tattersfield pulled his own sweater sleeve over his hand to get a better grip, and tugged upwards, releasing the fork. He instantly dropped it and walked off. Monaghan covered the wounds with his fingers but blood continued to trickle through the cracks. I was feeling faint myself at this point and I wondered how Monaghan was maintaining consciousness. I had never witnessed such brutality. I was relieved when he finally got to his feet, glared at us, and headed off to the toilets to clean himself up. I had assumed he would have headed straight to the deputy headmaster's office to report an attempted murder, with malice of forethought.

Ironically, Monaghan got through the afternoon without any teacher commenting on his blood-encrusted shirt and by the time he was getting on the school bus, he was already randomly punching, ear-flicking and spitting on the lower-schoolers, who had recently witnessed his stabbing.

When I got home, I told Andrew about the fight. He had already heard the exaggerated version through the rumour-mill. It was astonishing to hear how reports had changed in that short amount of time. His version involved Monaghan picking on Tattersfield and Jenkinson stepping in and stabbing Monaghan repeatedly in the throat with a fork. I corrected that but then we got into a deeper conversation about bullies and victims. Andrew was at his best when philosophising.

"Why is Monaghan such a bully?" I asked

"He gets bullied as much as he bullies," Andrew explained adding, "Monaghan's a victim." Andrew had obviously given it some serious thought.

"Let me ask you this. You know how some kids called him Frankenstein, because he has a square face?"

"Yes," I concurred.

"What would you do if somebody called you Frankenstein?" he asked.

I thought hard about it and gave him my honest answer, "I'd probably make a joke of it, heist up my shoulders and stagger around like Frankenstein."

"Exactly," he said, "Would it bother you?"

"Well if I looked like Frankenstein, it might," I quipped.

"No, you wouldn't let it bother you because you know that 'sticks and stones may break my bones….'" he said.

"…. but names will never hurt me." I finished his sentence.

"Exactly, but Monaghan doesn't get that. He thinks that the only way to stop taunting is to 'throw a wobbly,' which is pure entertainment to the bully. It's the same with your friend, Tattersfield." he explained.

"He's no friend of mine," I hastened to add.

"Well, that's his problem. Tattersfield has no friends. He has no clue how to make friends, or interact with friends," Andrew said rather piously. Like he had room to talk because I'd heard my brother tell Monaghan to 'Bugger off!' on numerous occasions. However, I had profound respect for my brother's wisdom and I mulled it over all night long. Maybe I could help Tattersfield by being his friend. Better still, I could teach him how to not be a victim, to use humour to diffuse situations. So, the next day, I pledged to myself that I was going to give Tattersfield a chance, after all he had impressed me for a brief time, heroically removing the pitch-fork from Frankenstein's neck, as the legend was starting to grow.

The next day, in Physics class, we were supposed to work in groups of three or four, to carry out an experiment to show the Principle of Moments. It was quite a tricky experiment which needed a person to hang a weight each side of a meter rule, suspended from a bulldog clip. Then the distance of each weight from the pivot needed to be recorded. It really was a four-person job and so I called Tattersfield over, to join me, Trainor and Jethro Stone.

"Bugger off, Tattersfield!" Stone instinctively retorted.

"We need him," I interjected and Stone eventually acquiesced. Jethro was nicknamed after a Beverly Hillbilly. He had an extraordinarily large head and had been the target of prior bullying. However, it forged no empathetic feelings with Tattersfield. In fact, he seemed to have less tolerance to Tattersfield than any of us.

"Tatty," I called him, despite the eye-rolling of the rest of the group, "hold this weight here, until I tell you to let go."

He obediently followed, with an *"Is this a trick?"* look on his face. It worked well and not only did the teacher congratulate us as being the first to finish, our graphs confirmed that we had the most accurate results. I think that he was pleased that we had been openly kind to Tattersfield and it was his subliminal way of rewarding us.

The next day, Tattersfield appeared with us at smoker's corner.

"Bugger off, Tattersfield," Jimmy Ellis instinctively blurted out.

"No, he's okay, Jim," I said, turning to Tattersfield and saying, "Crash the ash." Sure enough, he pulled out a pack of twenty Embassy King Size, and offered me, Jimmy and Darren Bolton a cigarette. My newfound alliance was paying off, Tatty was so eager to join the in-crowd he was willing to buy our friendship. My friends were surprised but went along with it.

"You ever had a girl, Tattersfield?" Bolton asked. We often fantasized about what we would do with a girl but I think my Top Rank snogging was about the extent of all our experiences combined.

"Yeah, I've had loads of 'em," Tattersfield lied. He could hardly get a boy to talk to him, never mind a girl.

"Oh yeah," Jimmy Ellis butted in, "did you use a Johnny?"

"Yeah, I always use Johnnies?" he dug himself deeper.

"What were their names? Bolton went on.

"Durex," Tattersfield responded.

Everyone laughed, which broke the tension of the inquisition. It gave me the opportunity to illustrate to Tattersfield how humour was the most powerful defence mechanism of all.

"Durex, that's a pretty name for a girl," I joked, "did you rubb-er up?" The others thought that this was hilarious and Tattersfield should have realized that I was rescuing him from making any more of a fool of himself.

But instead he turned on me and said, "Durex is a kind of Johnny you dick. Just because you've never had a girl doesn't mean I haven't!"

Now, that got under my skin particularly. We all knew one another were virgins but it was like an unwritten law that we never admitted it. Secondly, he had called me a dick in front of my friends, which was seriously overstepping the line. They all looked to me for a reaction. The first thing to come to mind was to say, *'Bugger off, Tattersfield,'* but I quickly remembered Andrew's 'sticks and stones' lecture. My friends were needing a response, and I could not be bested by Tattersfield. After all he had called me a dick.

I needed a good comeback and then it came to me. "You wouldn't know a dick, if you discovered one in your underpants, Tattersfield," I joked.

Ellis and Bolton laughed so hard they both started coughing up smoke. Again, Tattersfield could have rescued his position with a smile but his response was the uncoolest thing he could possibly have retorted as his social awkwardness hit a new low.

He declared, "I have a dick in my pants!"

"Oh yeah? Who's dick is it?" said Jimmy Ellis with a hilarious coup de grace.

The humiliation would have kept a lesser victim away from smoker's corner for evermore but, low and behold, Tattersfield was 'crashing the ash' to us all again at lunchtime.

Once we were lit, Jimmy started on Tattersfield's smoking technique. We had all known the pain of learning to inhale - the light-headedness and nausea were a rite of passage for novice smokers.

"You're not even inhaling that," Jimmy commented, as he took a deep lungful to illustrate the proper technique.

Tattersfield followed suit, and coughed uncontrollably. We all laughed because we knew what was coming next.

"Got to kill all the ciliated epithelial cells, mate," Darren Bolton told him, doing an inhalation demonstration of his own.

Tattersfield smiled, taking Bolton's use of the word 'mate' to be a term of endearment, rather than the condescension that was its true intent. He tried again and held the smoke for a bit longer before the cough reflex kicked in.

"There's no gain without pain, mate," Bolton told him, dragging once more on his own ciggie.

This was peer pressure in its essence. We were introducing an addiction to Tattersfield that might one day kill him, never mind his cilia. I suddenly had the thought that were attempting murder. Admittedly, less blatant than Jenko's attack on Monaghan's life but gradual murder, nonetheless. I did not hold that thought for long before I saw Tattersfield turn an insipid green before my very eyes. It was the inevitable nicotine nausea, that we had all experienced before. Nicotine was an acquired taste. Next thing, Tattersfield was vomiting, like a heroin addict trying 'smack' for the first time. With perseverance, the nausea would subside and the coughing would stop, once the ciliated epithelia were paralyzed. Then he would be one of us, a smoker. At this point, the lure was to hang out with the cool kids. Soon his body would be motivated by an entirely different force: addiction.

Tattersfield kept us in cigarettes for a couple of days and he started to gain mastery over the art of smoking, which should have given him some kudos. However, The Tattersfield Project was starting to look like a big mistake.

Firstly, he tried to give me a nickname. "Wanna fag, Twink?" he said out-of-the-blue.

126

"Who are you talking to, Tattersfield?" I asked, taking a cigarette. I could not believe that he had the audacity to try and nickname me.

"Don't you like it, Twink?" he said again.

"Don't ever call me that again!" I told him. He knew that I was serious from my tone and he went silent. Familiarity had bred contempt, just as in the saying. I thought that I had effectively nipped it in the bud.

Then Jimmy Ellis said, "Crash the ash, Tatty," deliberately highlighting the point that I had previously nicknamed Tattersfield. I hoped that Tattersfield did not pick up on this. Then Ellis turned to me and said, "Gotta light, Twink?" It was a living nightmare.

But then Tattersfield did the unthinkable. He grabbed the half-smoked cigarette, directly from my mouth, and held out the red end to Jimmy's cigarette. That crossed the line and I was almost ready to punch Tattersfield.

Jimmy sensed my annoyance and diffused the situation by taking my cigarette off Tattersfield, handing it back to me and leaning toward the end with his cigarette. "Thanks Mart," he made a point of saying, letting me know that the nickname game was exhausted.

Empowering Tattersfield had been a very regrettable experiment and he did not wait long to push me again. On the school bus home Tattersfield was on the seat behind me, when he inexplicably leaned over and grabbed my bus pass out of my blazer pocket. It was a liberty beyond belief.

"Give that back, Tattersfield!" I yelled. He tried to pass it back over his shoulder, to the kids behind, and I could see Monaghan salivating back there, desperate to get his pervy hands on my bus pass. I jumped up to follow my pass which was making a beeline for Frankenstein Monaghan. I had lost a bus pass once before and the replacement system was devised to deliberately be tiresome. It was almost in Monaghan's grip when Andrew's hand appeared and grabbed it.

"Piss off, Monaghan!" Andrew said, showing me how to maintain the pecking order. He handed the pass back to me, and looked me in the eye. Without a word, his eyes were telling me what to do. As the bus stopped Tattersfield raced to the doors and I raced after him. I caught Tattersfield about twenty feet from a church yard wall. I grabbed his blazer lapels and launched him over the wall and into a laurel bush.

"Sod off, Tattersfield," I cried, as he flew through the air.

The crowd behind me cheered, at what appeared to be an act of bullying but was actually an act of redemption. Order was restored.

Chapter 11: The Football Team

Green seemed to plague my entire life when it came to school houses. In Junior School, they named the houses after the four valleys: Dove, Churnet, Derwent and Manifold, were represented by red, blue, green and yellow. I was in Derwent, the crappiest of all the valleys and houses. Then I moved to Hartley High and four famous ex-students carried the same colours. I was in Wardle -greens. Whatismore, I was the only half-decent athlete in the whole team, so we came last in everything from cross-country running to table tennis. Our football team was the biggest joke, with Fatty Witherspoon in goals and not a single member of the school team, other than me.

For the school team trials, we had to play for our houses, which seemed unfair because our game was against Mitchell, the blues, who had Barry Cooper, Rob Bobbington and Lee Anderson all from the Staffordshire schoolboys team, and they made complete monkeys of us. I only really got an opportunity to show my speed when I received the ball from a kick-off and went full pelt down the wing. I saw Anderson heading to cut me off and found an extra gear, pushing the ball past him and driving for the line. Unfortunately, the fact that I had beaten Anderson for pace did not sit well with him and he slid in with both legs, so that my legs buckled under me at top speed. I rolled over and over, as the momentum carried me. It was a blatant foul but Anderson thought I'd been embellishing with my "Oscar winning performance" as he called it. So, every time I got the ball, he hacked my legs from under me. It was awful because he had been one of my heroes and I had started the day, proud to be on the same field. By the end of the match, I could not wait to get off the field.

However, when the school team was announced, I was astonished to be on the team sheet. I was to play left wing. I think Barry Cooper had put in a good word for me. Our first game was at Altringham on a Saturday morning. We won 18-0, which sounds like it would be terrific but it was boring. Altringham had no fight, whatsoever, and on one occasion Bobbington dribble the ball to their goal, stopped on the line, and got down on his knees so that he could head it over the line. The next week was at home and we won 14-1, and the one was an embarrassing own goal resulting from a firmly struck back pass to an unprepared goalie.

It was not until our third match that we had viable opposition. Denstone college was a private boarding school and their team were so welcoming it was deceptive. I had always found the natural confidence and politeness of boarding school students to be beguiling. There was a naivety that came from protection from the real world. It never occurred to them that there were children who resented their privilege and they were oblivious to the reverse snobbery that our players brought with them. All their players insisted on shaking hands with all our players along with the referee, which I worked out to be a hundred and forty-four handshakes. This created the illusion that they were going to be a load of namby-pambies and that the Altringham record was in danger.

However, as soon as that whistle blew they were transformed into a football machine. When we had the ball they all took up defensive stances and man marked us tightly until we relinquished possession. As soon as they got the ball they worked so hard 'off the ball' so that they always had passing options. Meanwhile, our defence ran around like headless chickens chasing the ball all over the place. I saw Anderson and Bobbington close ranks and try to rough them up a little by tackling from behind. It was only Rob Jones' heroic saves that kept us with a fighting chance.

Lee Anderson gave away a blatant penalty just before half-time, and the opposing attacker apologized to Anderson for not remaining on his feet when Andie's high speed two-footed special had chopped him down. Then he placed the ball on the penalty spot and did something I've never seen before. Jones feigned to dive left, hoping to trick the penalty-taker, and then leapt full length right. However, the shooter, cool as a cucumber, hit the ball right down the middle. He had banked on the goalie diving one way or the other and vacating the middle lane. It was just being practical but Jones was humiliated.

At half time, Rocky Timpson, our 'coach,' gathered us in a huddle and gave us a pep talk. "Okay guys, you are the better players but they are the better team. Learn from them! Whenever we have the ball everyone should run into a position where they can receive the ball. And talk to each other. When they have the ball, hassle them. Anderson, you're doing a fantastic job but keep it clean! Wells, you're the fastest man on the field. Stay on the wing, don't come inside. And when you get the ball take it to the corner and cross it. Okay?" I nodded in agreement. He continued, "Everybody else, Wells is our secret weapon so feed him the ball. Now let's go!"

It was an inspiring team talk, at least for me. I was unaware that Rocky had even noticed my speed. He had also done me no harm with my teammates, lifting me to 'secret weapon' status. Straight from the kick-off, our players started to work harder off-the-ball and there was constant dialogue.

"Cooper," I yelled, when he had the ball but by the time he looked up their left back was on me.

"Man on," yelled Bobbington. alerting Cooper to an oncoming tackle, which Cooper side-stepped.

I wanted to run inside and offer myself but I remembered that Rocky was insistent that my job was to cling to the side-line. I was momentarily free and I shouted, "Cooper, wing it!" but again, by the time he had glanced over, the left back was all over me. The flaw in the 'talking' was that the opposition could also hear it. So, I decided to stay quiet and hope the team had their 'secret weapon' in mind. I spent the next five minutes uninvolved, watching from the edge of the field, which was an experience. Sure enough, our players were suddenly starting to click. They played in small triangles, so that our man on the ball always had choices. Finally, Anderson intercepted a ball and looked over to the right wing. I timed a run and Anders' shouted "Wells," and lofted a perfectly weighted ball about twenty yards ahead of me. I was away in a flash and reached the by-line so quickly that I had to wait for the rest of the field to catch up. Eventually, I crossed a ball exactly onto the penalty spot, where Cooper was bearing down. He caught the ball right on the laces and it rocketed into the top right-hand corner. We were level.

Our goal seemed to shock the Denstone players and they stepped up their game, bringing a couple of miraculous saves out of Jones. Then, in a carbon copy of the first half, Anderson gave away another penalty and the same player stepped up to take it.

It was a game of psychology. Surely, he would not try the same trick again? Jones would not be fooled twice. Although, that would be a tremendous bluff. If I was taking the penalty I would remember that Jones had feigned to his left and gone right. Therefore, it would be best to shoot to his left. The penalty-taker took a longer run-up, suggesting that he was planning a hard strike. Jones took an initial step to the left, and the striker must have thought like me because he drove the ball hard and low to the goalie's left. However, all three of us were on the same wavelength because Jones continued his dive and his strong left-hand tipped the ball onto the post. Luckily, Cooper was alert enough to be following in and he managed to clear the rebound from danger. It was brilliant, and it lifted the whole team.

As players began to tire, the man-to-man marking became slacker and when Cooper received the ball in midfield he saw me start my wing run. He floated the ball with some side-spin over the heads of the defence and suddenly I was all alone bearing down on goal. I had almost too much time to think about what to do. I had dreamed of this position many times with the goalkeeper coming out to narrow the angle. Should I lob the ball over the goalie, blast it past him when he was close, or take the ball around him? I opted for the last choice and my speed carried me gracefully past him, with the empty net beckoning. I kept my concentration, planted my standing leg and was about to sweep the ball into the net when I felt both the goalkeeper's hands gripping my ankles. I was literally rooted to the spot as the whistle blew for a penalty.

Rob Bobbington was our designated penalty taker but he first offered me the ball. I was tempted but I knew that Rocky would be mad if we ignored the plans. If psychology had played a part in the second penalty, then it was doubly true, now. Bobbo' usually just put the ball down and blasted it. However, there was far more pressure on this kick. He took his time placing it and took his usual run up. Their goalkeeper launched himself to his left and Bobbington stroked the ball right down the middle repeating the opposition's goal. It was a stroke of brilliance and they had no time to strike back, as the final whistle blew straight after play had resumed.

The Denstone boys were not familiar with the sensation of losing but they rapidly resumed their composure. Their captain led the three cheers for Hartley High and they all applauded us off the field. Three lessons were learned that day - the importance of teamwork, a plan, and how to be magnanimous in defeat.

Chapter 12: Downing

If we had known that Christmas 1966 would be our last one in Sutton Green we would probably have made more fuss. We should have known because Nana Lena had already told dad that she wanted to give him the necessary twenty percent deposit to buy a house. My parents had made several offers but everything seemed to fall through. The first house was in Bucknall, right next to the school. It seemed to really appeal to mum, to have us within walking distance of school but dad finally decided that it was too far from his work. Ironically, he approved of a bid on a house in Ash Bank, which was even further away.

However, his boss, who owned a mansion in Endon called Blackwood Hall, advised him to buy something as expensive as he could afford. This was based on the theory that inflation would soon make the mortgage payments affordable. Dad took the advice and decided that the Ash Bank house was too unambitious. Mum had her heart set on that house because it had an elongated back garden. Also, she was booked into Hayward hospital to have her varicose veins stripped and she would be out-of-action until a week before, Christmas for any further house-hunting escapades.

My second favourite teacher, Downing, taught biology. He happened to be teaching us about the circulatory system, so when he mentioned veins a light bulb went off in my head. I raised my hand.

"What Wells?" he said impatiently.

"Please sir, what are varicose veins?" I asked.

I think he had been expecting some smartarse question because he rolled his eyes sarcastically at first and said, "What do you want to know that for?"

I blushed, suddenly feeling that I should not be talking about my mum's problem in front of the class. So, I clammed up and said, "Don't know, sir."

"You don't know?" he responded, meaning that I was supposed to know my reason for asking.

"No sir, that's why I'm asking," I retorted. Now I was being a smartarse and some of the class snickered. That awkward streak, as my mum called it, had plagued me throughout life. Knowing when to keep quiet was never my strength and I could see that I had annoyed him. I was also beginning to suspect that he did not know what varicose veins were because he never did address my question.

Twenty minutes later, in the same lesson, Darren Trainor whispered, do you think Downing's wearing a toupee? I had noticed he was doing something different with his hair. It was usually gassed back with Brylcream but it was grease-free, on this day.

"Downing's got a wig on, Downing's got a wig on," whispered Trainor. As only Trainor could, this made me crack up, and Downing was on me in a flash.

"What are you laughing at Wells?" he demanded.

"Nothing sir," I told him. I was certainly not planning on embarrassing him by revealing his 'wig' to the class.

"Come out here, Wells, "he summoned, beckoning me to his platform behind the demonstration bench. He was smiling, which I had learned was often the precursor to persecution; I cringed as the class chuckled and he asked, "Do you always laugh at nothing, Wells?"

"No sir," I responded

"No sir?" he repeated rhetorically.

"Sometimes I laugh at something sir, but this time I was laughing at nothing," my awkward streak told him, almost involuntarily.

"Put your head under this tap, Wells," he insisted, helping me by grabbing my ear for guidance.

I obliged.

"Do you know what they do to people who laugh at nothing, Wells?" he asked, as the whole class giggled.

"Brainwash them, sir?" I said, anticipating that he was about to turn the tap on me. I thought that he would have laughed, because he was obviously enjoying entertaining my peers.

However, he was the funny man and I was his stooge in this situation. The class went silent, awaiting his next move.

"Men in white coats put you in strait jackets," he laughed. Then he launched into a novelty song that was in the hit parade. "They're coming to take me away, ha ha, hee hee, ho ho, to the funny farm........" I began to stand up, thinking that he had finished humiliating me and this caused his mood to change. "Where are you going, Wells?" he yelled, pushing my head back down.

"Don't know, sir." I automatically said.

"Are you going to tell me why you were laughing?" he asked, making clear this was his ultimate request.

I still knew that it would be unwise to tell the truth so I said, "No sir." This was the signal to switch on the water. He turned it on hard and it gushed in my ear and hair and ran down the side of my face, up my nostrils. The class were in hysterics as I walked back to my desk, dripping like a drowned rat.

For some reason, Downing seemed to respect that I had not 'cracked' under his water torture and he was always pleasant with me from that point on. I told Andrew about the episode and he just laughed. Downing's son, Oscar Downing, was in my brother's class. In fact, they were close friends, so I think that something must have been said, through the grapevine. It did not look good that Downing had taken a genuine inquiry from a student, who was worried about his mum's upcoming operation, and turned it into a public humiliation. Downing started the next lesson with a statement.

"Wells, you were a good sport, last period," he started. "Anyway, with all the water sports, I forgot to answer your question about varicose veins."

"I know, sir," I said politely, not wanting to relive the episode. His kindness revealed that his son must have filtered the story, omitting the toupee part and focusing on my worries about my mum's imminent hospitalization.

"So," he said, "you remember that I told you that veins have backflow valves?"

The whole class nodded in unison, determined to keep on his good side.

"Well, sometimes these valves get clogged so they don't get closed properly and deoxygenated blood stays in them. What colour is deoxygenated blood, Wells?" he suddenly asked.

"Blue, sir," I answered.

"Good. So, these veins get wide because they are filled with bluish blood from the leaky valves," he explained. "Sometimes people have a tiny operation to strip the faulty valves out. It's a very safe procedure."

"Thank you, sir," I replied. It was not an apology, as such. It was better. I suspected that he had gone off and read up on them but more impressive was the way he had discreetly reassured me.

I was just starting to find newfound respect for Downing, when he said, "Now, which one's Trainor?"

Darren raised his hand.

"Okay, Mr Trainor, I believe you have a theory?"

"No, sir," he replied, going as red as his own hair.

"Come out here, boy, "Downing insisted. Trainor went slowly out. He was not used to the limelight and no teachers ever experienced his wicked sense of humour directly.

"Give it a tug, son," he insisted, leaning forward so his new ungreased hairstyle was almost touching Trainor's hand. A collective gasp skipped around the class. By now Trainor had had the whole school convinced that he was wearing a hairpiece. He knew that there was not an option, so he grabbed Downing's hair and pulled very gently, then progressively harder until it was apparent that it was not a wig. Downing had simply joined the Beatle-loving generation, about three-years late.

"Satisfied?" grinned the teacher.

"Yes sir, I mean no sir," answered the flummoxed Trainor. There really was no right answer.

"Whilst we are on the subject of hair," Downing continued," what kind of hair-dye do you use?"

"None sir, this is my natural colour," Trainor responded.

"Wells," Downing shouted, checking my level of attention.

"Yes sir," I retorted, enjoying the situation far more than the previous lesson.

"How can we test whether this is his natural hair colour or not?" he quizzed.

"Use a solvent, sir," I remembered.

Downing openly laughed, "Ha ha, very good Wells. Can you remind the class of the universal solvent?"

"Water sir," I replied, at which Downing grabbed Trainor's neck and thrust his head under the same tap that had drenched me, a couple of days earlier.

"Water indeed, Wells!" he concurred as Trainor writhed under the gushing flow. "Well, it seems like Mr. Trainor was telling the truth!"

When he re-joined me at my desk, Trainor whispered under his breath, "Bugger."

"What was that, Trainor?" Downing asked.

I jumped in to his rescue, "He says that he was glad to assist you in the demonstration, sir."

Trainor nodded passively and Downing flashed his demonic smile, which made kids love him and fear him simultaneously.

Chapter 13: Varicose veins

Haywood Hospital was like something from the previous century, compared with the ultra-modern North Staffs Royal Infirmary. However, it had that unique small-town camaraderie that served as a welcome mat, particularly with all the Christmas streamers and tinsel-covered Christmas tree. Once dad had ensured that mum had recovered from the anaesthetic, he saw his visiting duties as complete. He focused on the house-hunting each day, while we took turns to take care of Eric, during the Christmas holidays.

One day, Andrew took Eric Christmas shopping, leaving me to believe that he was probably going to get me a present. Dad had gone to view a house in Penkville, closer to his work and I decided to set off to Haywood Hospital. I could not afford the standard gift of flowers or grapes but I scraped together enough money for a Bournville dark chocolate bar, which I knew to be her favourite. When I arrived, I was welcomed by a flurry of nurses who made a huge fuss of me, which I enjoyed immensely. Mum had not expected a visit but she was positively bristling with pride. And when I pulled out the chocolate bar there was an audible swooning in the room.

"Oh Beryl, he's precious," said the Ward Sister, who had been summoned specially to meet me.

"He's going to break some hearts, Bet," said another nurse.

"He already is, Eva," she said, "he's at that Top Rank every Saturday." I was hoping that she was not going to reveal what she knew about my Top Rank snogging exploits. She looked like she was about to spill the beans and I felt a blush welling. However, she checked herself, with a sort of, 'I'll tell you later,' look, much to my relief.

"I've been learning about varicose veins at school," I explained. I told her about what Downing had taught me about the valves and deoxygenated blood.

"Handsome and clever," commented Eva.

"I'm very lucky, Eve," she replied. It was really refreshing to be described in this way. Andrew was usually the family flagship, when it came to looks or brains. I was half expecting her to bring him up at that moment but she was happy to let me take the limelight.

Whilst I was enjoying the attentions of the ward, unbeknownst to mum, dad was making a decision that would change out family forever. The house in Penkville was ideal. It had three bedrooms, three stories, with a couple of playrooms and a double garage in the basement. The garden was a massive landscaped expanse. It had rolling lawns and huge rockeries everywhere. The owners were selling up and moving to America, so they had priced it for a quick sale. There were allegedly three more families booked to visit it after him. So, he made a snap decision and offered four thousand eight hundred pounds.

"Tell you what, for another two hundred, we will leave all the beds, furniture, and everything," said Mrs Cooper, the owner. They shook hands and by that evening, dad was showing us around our new home. It was splendid.

The next day he went to visit mum at the Hospital and told her that he had bought a house. She was both elated and livid. It was three days later when we finally picked her up from hospital and took her to view our new place. She then understood that he had no choice. For once in his life, his gamble had paid off, he had more than 'broken even;' she fell instantly in love with the place. It was the best Christmas present, beyond her wildest dreams. That was not to say that she did not retain her right to future righteous indignation about her exclusion from the decision. I felt for her on that front until Andrew, in his ultimate wisdom, pointed something out.

"Finally, mum gets to have her cake and eat it, too," he told me. It was his favourite proverb.

"How do you mean?" I asked. I was familiar with the saying but did not see how it applied in this context.

He elaborated, "Well, she gets to enjoy all the good things about the house, and blame dad for anything that goes wrong, from plumbing to squeaky furniture." I saw that, since a big part of the family dynamic was blame apportionment. So, in a way it was 'the gift that kept giving.'

The last Christmas in Sutton Green was an odd affair. Firstly, ours was the best council house on the block, with a big corner plot back garden and a garage; not to mention a much-desired blue door. People knew that the Stevensons, who were the previous tenants, had tipped off dad about their leaving. He charmed the clerk into rubber-stamping his application. So, when word got out that we were moving, people were scrambling to get my dad to bequeath the plot to them. They were barking up the wrong tree because the council clerk was the one with the power but dad took great delight milking the neighbours. Dad did have a way of making everyone he knew (except for mum) feel that they had a special understanding. Barry Pratt's dad was the first to knock.

146

"Hey Pete, fancy a pint at the Berwick?" George Pratt asked. He had never drunk with my dad before so his intentions were far from subtle.

"I can do you a quick one, George," dad replied, donning his coat and scarf. An hour later the two were meandering up the road smelling of two or three pints.

"Okay Peter, do you think ten's, enough?" he asked. My assumption was that he was talking about pound notes, until he turned up from his work the next evening with ten cardboard packing boxes.

Later that night, Mrs Tinsley, the next-door neighbour tapped timidly on the door.

Mum answered, "Hiya Hilda."

"Good evening, Beryl, is Pete in?"

Dad joined her at the front door. "Don't tell me, you want to move?"

"No Pete," she responded, "I just want to make sure that you don't let the Walkers, across the street have it. I couldn't bare having them live next door." They really were the most abysmal family. They had a motor-bike and sidecar, which had been known to transport all seven family members. Without a silencer, the motor-bike kept the whole estate appraised of the entire family's whereabouts. Late one evening I looked out of my window to see the twenty-two-year-old daughter stooping on the pavement, in front of their house. Then a stream of pee trickled down the gradient in front of her. Then she tried to stand up, lost her balance and rolled into her own urine. Her little sister was only three years old and she was like a miniature version of her. Unfortunately, she never seemed to speak. It was hard to tell whether she had impediment or whether she was just extremely quiet.

They had three brothers. There was a twenty-year-old, who had some sort of problem, where he kept fanning himself with a stick or pencil or anything he happened to have in his hand. He was often mocked by the local kids and he would get mad and try and chase them, which was quite disturbing to watch. His two younger brothers were high school aged but they spent most of their time away, presumably at Borstal. Ironically, the most popular band in the country were called The Walker Brothers. They had a song called "The Sun Ain't Gonna Shine Anymore," which raced through the mind of every person on the estate, whenever they ventured out of the house.

The two parents never stopped yelling at each other. Even when they were not angry, which was rare, they still spoke in booming voices. Perhaps the motorbike had taken its toll?

Dad assured our neighbour, "Well, I can promise they won't hear anything from me, Anne," dad assured her.

"I don't want the Foots either," she added.

The Foot family were odd. Mrs Foot was a close friend of our previous neighbour, 'Sparky Ears' Johnson. They were the biggest gossips in the road. Mrs Foot never had a good word to say about anybody and she was highly competitive. Whenever horse and carts came up the street, whether they were rag-and-bone men, or coal men, Mrs Foot would race out with a shovel and gather up horseshit for her roses. Even though nobody else had any interest in it, she clutched her shovel as though she would have fought to the death. Her 19-year-old son was known estate-wide as a pervert. Andrew, Barry and I, had both made mistakes, when we were younger of accepting lifts off him in his 3-wheeler Reliant car. He carried magazines with naked women in his glove compartment and had a standard routine of taking them out and being creepy. Her 21-year-old son was probably okay. His only sin was to look exactly like his pervy younger brother. Both were obese and sweaty.

Dad assured her that he would not let the Foots know about the vacancy either. As soon as she left, Tina Carolla's mum, who was pregnant from a third different man according to what Mrs Foot told Sparky Ears, tapped on the door. When dad opened it, I watched her hard face soften, and her Dusty Springfield eyelashes spring into seductive mode. I had never seen her behave that way with my mum.

"Oh Peter, I'm glad I caught you, I've bought some chocolates for the kids Christmas stockings" she rasped, in what I believed to be an Ertha Kitt impression, she handed over two boxes of chocolate liquors, which Andrew grabbed before our parents noticed the inappropriateness, of the gift. "I was wondering if anybody has asked you about the house yet?"

"No but I'll mention you're interested if you like," he told her. Then mum appeared at the door and dad hastened the conversation. "So, thanks for the kids' gifts," he said, adding "and congratulations on the baby."

"What baby?" she replied, and then held her face just long enough to see dad squirm, and then she smiled saying, "had you going didn't I?"

"That you did," dad laughed with embarrassment. She was not attractive but her personality seemed to captivate every male she met, and repel women to the same degree. As soon as he closed the door, mum wiped the look off dad's face with her own disapproving glare.

"Who's she kidding? She must be eleven months pregnant," mum said.

"I thought it only took nine months.........oh I get it!" I said, suddenly feeling stupid.

There were also a few inquiries from strangers from other parts of the estate, and dad tactfully made them all feel that they had equal chance. Unbeknownst to anyone, the council had earmarked the house to be the first on a refurbishment regime and their dreams of moving into the house that was once inhabited by the Wells family remained unfulfilled. There were so many variables and nobody ever quite knew the rules when it came to council decisions.

Chapter 14: Past, Present and Future Presents

There was a piece of furniture that I had noticed in our home-to-be, that I was most thrilled about inheriting. It was a stereo record player that dad called a Plusogram, for some inexplicable reason. Once I had established that this move was happening and not another red herring, I had an excuse to buy Andrew the most awesome Christmas present: his first record.

In mid-December, on the same day that dad was buying our new house in Penkville, an even greater life-moulding event was occurring simultaneously: Jimi Hendrix released a single, called Hey Joe. Not many people had heard of him. However, Andrew had read in New Musical Express about this guitar genius, who was taking the London scene by storm. Apparently, all the coolest people, like Eric Clapton and George Harrison were turning up to the clubs to see the instant legend. They were simply drooling at the orgasmic sounds Jimi was thrashing from his Fender Stratocaster. My brother Andrew, who initially introduced The Beatles to my world, was now heralding Jimi as the rock Messiah.

As well as musical liberation, 1966 had brought freedoms to the whole family. Mum's emancipation came through her job, her ability to drive and the last untouched taboo for her to gain some parity with my dad's mother, the dreaded Nana Lena.

Her early years had been taunted by this woman, who made it clear that she did not feel that my mum was good enough for her son. Lena was an outright bully. However, as mum's confidence grew her response to bullying evolved from one of appeasement to one of confrontation. The worm turned!

Now, I'm not sure whether this was just a miscalculation, or an act of passive aggressiveness but my mum decided that Lena should finally get a substantial Christmas present from us. Lena had a weird combination of personality traits, on top of her already established bully persona, she could also be described as a generous narcissist. She loved to give things away, just to impress the receivers, that she had affluence. Unfortunately, she often forgot where the gifts had come from. On the previous Christmas, mum had bought her a huge basket of Estee Lauder soaps and lotions but by March dad was carrying them into our house.

152

"My mother wondered if you could use these dear?" he said, unaware that she had lovingly selected then for Lena a couple of months earlier.

"I wonder why she would think that?" mum snapped, bringing a look of confusion to dad's face.

"I think it's really expensive stuff, dear," he said, adding insult to injury.

"I think you might be right," she responded, walking the whole basket, with bows still intact, straight to the outside dustbin. The crash of the dustbin lid left us all in no doubt that the conversation was over but dad never discovered why mum was so offended by his mother's generosity.

So, for Christmas 1966, mum decided that Lena needed a new pet. I had to believe that it was meant as a gesture of kindness to a lonely woman. Lena had lost her little French poodle, Ricky, earlier that year. She had adored him, despite his interminable snappiness. When mum was consoling her, they had a conversation that she would never have another dog which mum read as 'I'd like a cat, one day.' Mum decided that Christmas was that day. So, two days before Christmas, mum prepared a box by wrapping it with seasonal paper and making a few air holes. We picked up the most delightful Seal Point Siamese kitten, popped it in the box and headed to Lena's.

As soon as mum and I pulled up onto the drive of Lena's luxury bungalow, the door was flung open and her eyes lit up when she saw the present in my arms. I was given the honour of carrying in the substantially large present.

"Come on in," she insisted, planting an Estee Lauder-flavoured peck on my cheek before I had chance to duck. "I'll put the kettle on, and Martin you can pop that present under the tree in the living room," she insisted.

I was dutifully following this direction when mum said, "No, Lena this is something you will want to open right away. This is so much better than the gift we gave you last year."

We watched Lena's expression of puzzlement as she was obviously wracking her brains to try and remember last year's gift.

"No Bet, I'll open it on Christmas morning, if it's all the same to you. Take it through Martin," she insisted, with a little more annoyance in her voice.

"No Mart, she needs to open it now!" mum responded, matching her assertiveness. They both glared at me, as if it was my duty to choose a side, as I stood rooted to the spot. Both had a history of bullying me and where mum's attacks were more predictable, Lena's were fiercer. I was conflicted but then a tiny meowing sound emerged from the box and rescued me from my awkward position.

"Is it a cat? I don't want a cat!" my grandmother insisted.

"It's a kitten," mum responded, surprisingly unperturbed. "You will love her, once you see her.

Show her, Mart." She motioned for me to undo the present, which was starting to make a noise like a tiny baby. It would have melted any mother's heart in an instant but Lena was not known for her heart.

"Beryl I told you after Ricky died that I didn't want another pet." she reasoned.

"It's not a dog, Lena, it's just a sweet innocent kitten," said mum, still thinking that the animal's sheer cuteness would win her over.

"Take it away," she said.

So, mum then tried to appeal to her snob values by saying, "It cost a lot of money, Lena, it's a pedigree Siamese."

"I'll give you the money," said Lena opening her purse and pulling out a wad of twenty pounders. Sounded like a good deal to me and it seemed like the natural time to quit. However, mum was still sure that seeing the kitten would change Lena's mind.

"Open the box!" she ordered me. I looked over at Lena still clutching her wad of notes and it took me all my efforts not to complete a catchphrase by yelling, "Take the Money!" There was a TV quiz show called "Take your Pick," Where the audience used to yell these conflicting commands. "Open the box!...... Take the Money!"

Neither happened. Mum returned the kitten to the breeder, for half the initial price. A pedigree kitten is probably the worst Christmas present mum ever chose but at least it was memorable, unlike a basket of soap.

Chapter 15: Changes

I discreetly got puberty under my belt, early in the new year. Luckily this event passed unnoticed but some of my peers were less subtle. Toftie was unfortunate enough to share his transition to manhood in the middle of a *Ecouter, Regardez, Repeater* session. His voice cracked, like a saxophonist tuning up, as he was trying to say, "Janine coupe la carne a l'assiette," which meant that Trainor's fantasy girl was cutting up her meat on her plate.

"Sounds like Toftie's ready to start cutting up his meat," Trainor half-whispered in my ear. I know that Pedro heard him but decided that it was in everyone's interest to pretend that he had not. It made no difference because every phrase for the next two weeks involved thirty students doing an impression of Toftie's Doppler Effected descent into puberty.

An all-boys grammar school, riddled with pubescents was not a healthy environment for anyone with two X-chromosomes. Every staff member was male, all based on the premise that females would be a distraction. Ironically, the less academic students were considered fine to co-mingle, and my friends that attended those school seemed to have a far more respectful attitude to the opposite sex.

One day, a drama group came to perform for all the high schools in the area. Coach loads of sixth form girls, from the other local high schools, arrived in their droves. The hundred-yard march from outside the school gate, to the school hall must have felt like an eternity for the girls. It was as if the female equivalent of The Beatles was arriving, as five hundred lascivious boys lined the entire length of the entrance. The immaculate brown uniforms of the Brownhills girls were the first to be greeted by wolf-whistles. Every girl wore a brown beret, to compliment her matching blazer and skirt. Strict rules allowed the skirt to ride only four inches above the knee, but you could see that many of the girls had made some last-minute belt adjustments to exploit the situation.

Similarly, somebody must have sneaked a make-up bag onto the Thistley Hough coach because, despite the no makeup policy, the 'Thistles' contingent emerged from their coach looking more like Air Hostesses than schoolgirls. One girl had even tied her pale green blouse under her bosom, which seemed to accentuate her curves as well as revealing a bare flat stomach that left half the crowd gasping between whistles.

Some girls were milking the moment, but it looked like most of them would have welcomed it if the ground had opened and swallowed them without trace. Most of the girls' teachers realized that the testosterone-fuelled crowd was an animal best ignored. They focused their attention on their charges, with encouraging side-of-the-mouth comments such as, "Just ignore them ladies." Or "Eyes forward, girls."

However, one tweed-skirted mistress, who was probably well-respected for her tyranny in her own school, decided to tackle the obscene hysteria of boys.

"Gentlemen," she yelled in a stern voice, "that is enough!" There was a definite lull, as the boys shushed one another. She took this to mean that she was having an impact on our consciences. "This is a disgrace!" she added, making the girls with her blush even more than they were. The crowd went seriously quiet, at this point, all except Monaghan, who was so caught up in the moment, his voice continued over the lull.

"Get 'em off!" Monaghan shouted. I cringed in empathy with the girls.

Tweedy responded, "Young man, what do you have to say?"

"Sorry," would have been the obvious answer, but instead Monaghan said, "Thank you."

"Thank you? What do you mean, thank you?" she demanded.

"Thank you, miss," he added.

"What are you thanking me for, stupid boy? she asked, genuinely perplexed.

Then, an anonymous voice from the back helped him out.

"Thank you for the crumpet!" shouted the secret voice. Laughter erupted and Tweedy would have done best to cut her losses. That was what her girls wanted. Cut and run. Instead she marched into the crowd, demanding to know who shouted it.

Tweedy obviously had perfect control of teenagers in her own environment but the 'crumpet' comment had her truly flummoxed. She spun slowly around, trying to silence every boy with her penetrating glare. I felt her eye-contact with me for a split-second and a cold bolt shot down my spine, like I had just been touched by the Ice Queen. I looked away from her stare, only to realize that most of the boys were laughing at her. They obviously were not as used to a semi-psychotic mother, as was I. Then, in a sort of displacement reaction, Tweedy magically produced a six-inch ruler and spun around on her group of girls.

"Four inches, ladies. Skirts should be no higher than four inches above the knee." she announced.

If she could not exercise control of the boy's behaviour, her need for control was turned upon the girls. Now, in her own classroom, girls would have undoubtedly complied. Indeed, some were instinctively scrambling with their belts in desperate efforts to lower their hemlines. However, under the observance of a cheering crowd of gawping males, the annoying ruler suddenly seemed like a symbol of degradation.

"Get that thing away from me!" exclaimed a formally perfect student.

"Four inches, four inches," insisted the teacher.

"Four inches, four inches!" chanted the crowd of boys, clapping to the beat.

Instinct forced the humiliated "Thistles' girls to march with the beat, while Tweedy chased each of them with her ruler, involuntarily locked into her 'Four inches' mantra.

Meanwhile, one of the younger kids had made eye-contact with Monaghan, as they mouthed "four inches' which caused him to take offence and punch out. His fist only just missed the back of my head, causing me to recoil, setting up a chain reaction of movements which, on reflection, might have appeared like a mini-riot.

Suddenly, the girls were racing to the hall entrance, like they were about to be mobbed, with the teacher, ludicrously waving the ruler around her thighs.

By the time the Saint Peter's girls arrived, Fizzer was outside keeping order. He commanded the Coach driver, to drive his bus through the gates and right up to the school entrance, so the blue uniforms of Saint Peter's remained a mystery to our boys.

Boos and jeers rang out, as the disappointed, sex-starved, Hartley High schoolers were denied the much-anticipated Church of England crumpet.

Once the girls were safely inside, the crowd disperse into smaller groups, misinterpreting signals and embroidering stories about who fancied who, mainly based on imagined furtive glances. Jenko, who had taken to hanging around with us lower graders led us to the drama groups white van, which was filled with props. It was hard to decipher what sort of play they must have been performing as the props ranged from a milking stool to a couple of sword-fencing foils.

"Touchez," exclaimed Jenko, waving around the foil like he was a musketeer.

"Put it back, you'll get caned!" I whispered loudly.

Apparently, this was the wrong advice because it triggered him to set off over the fields, wafting his sword with complete abandon. I should have been perturbed, having witnessed his willingness to stab Monaghan with a fork but I just assumed that he would tire of the sword game and return it to the naively unsecured prop van.

It was not until the next day that Jenko approached me and Barry Pratt and offered to buy us each a 99, from Wrench. I accepted the offer instantly and was surprised when Barry declined, because he was normally more of a glutton than me. It was not until after I'd nearly completed the feast when Jenko revealed the true nature of his generosity.

"You two remember when I was playing with that sword yesterday?" he asked.

"Yes," I answered.

"No," the wiser Barry answered, at exactly the same time.

He turned to Barry, "You probably don't remember, Barry, because I only had it for a second and then put it straight back."

"That'll be it, " said Barry.

"Mart, you remember me putting it back, don't you?" insisted Jenko, watching the last lick of Wrench's vanilla elixir adhere to my tongue.

"Mmmmm," I responded, talking simultaneously to the ice cream and Jenkinson. That seemed enough for him.

"I'm glad I've got you two as witnesses," he revealed, "somebody must have taken it, after I put it back. Buggers are saying I took it!"

Barry shrugged, nonchalantly.

Jenko turned to me and I tried to reproduce Barry's gesture but it appeared more like incredulity than indifference.

"You're not going to let me down are you?" demanded Jenko.

I shook my head, feeling like I had just sold my soul to the Devil, for a sixpenny ice cream, with chocolate flake. If you could put a price on anxiety, then it would have needed more than fifty of Wrench's double flake specials to compensate me for the worry that Jenko had imposed on me.

If I got hauled into the Deputy Head's inquiry and lied, I would be guilty of aiding and abetting. If I 'let him down' and snitched I might end up with a fork in the neck or even impaled on the very weapon I had watched him steal.

In the past, I had had a hamster, named Whiskey, who lived in a cage in the garden shed. He was my confidante and the shed had been my confessional. Whenever I shared my worries with Whiskey, he used to listen intently, without comment, and he would often help me gain perspective on my unceasing problems. Unfortunately, Whiskey had died the previous year and he was never replaced. By all accounts, I had not cleaned his cage as frequently or thoroughly as I had initially agreed. Apparently, the whiff of hamster was not 'everyone's cup of tea.'

Whiskey had really been replaced by my journal but I was reluctant to incriminate myself too much in writing, since my mum had revealed her disrespect for my boundaries. But I had to process the event and I chose to encrypt some of the terminology. Instead of Sword, I picked the word cucumber. Jenko was substituted with monkey; ice cream became a banana; and fork was a ping-pong bat.

"I watched the monkey take the cucumber over the fields and then he bribed me with a banana. I can't let the monkey down or I'll end up impaled on a ping-pong bat, like Monaghan or even run through by a psychotic monkey's banana" said my journal.

"Let's see mum decipher that," I thought. The journaling served to focus my thoughts before my bedtime but without my hamster to bounce ideas off, the therapeutic side of the conversation was missing. So, my night was punctuated with tosses and turns and weird dreams about monkeys chasing me with forks. But the real nightmare occurred after I had awakened. In the middle of French class, the school secretary opened Pedro's door and asked if there was a Wells in the room.

During the walk, back to the deputy headmaster's office I could feel my heart pounding in my throat. At the same time, the adrenaline made me feel like I was going to throw up. After a couple of minutes, I saw Barry Pratt emerge from the office, looking as pale as I felt. He nodded surreptitiously but if he was trying to communicate instruction in his gesture I was missing it entirely.

"Wells?" said the kind voice of Mr. Lowe, who was mainly recognized as a caning machine. Not many boys emerged from his room without freshly whipped backsides. He beckoned me into his office and sat behind his desk while I fidgeted and squirmed on the spot. "Do you know why you're here?"

"No sir," I replied. I knew that his question was a famous ploy of policemen and teachers to get kids to self-incriminate.

"Do you know anything about a sword?" he asked. It was devilish because either a "Yes" or a "No" would draw me deeper into a web of deceit. I had also recently learned from Downing that "I don't know" was not an acceptable way to plead the fifth.

So, I stood uncomfortable, silent for what seemed like the longest time. If only I could have worked out what Barry had told him. Barry and I had been friends for years and had had times when we were younger where we felt almost psychically-linked. I tried to remember the micro-glance that he gave me. My instinct said that he had held out but for what?

The deputy was obviously very comfortable with awkward silences, watching kids squirm until they cracked.

"Well?" he said, still suggesting that he had a heart, despite his flogging prowess. Then, a great clarity came to me, as if I had consulted with

Whiskey himself. This man was not my tormentor. It was Jenko who was the tormentor.

"Sir, I think he might kill me if I tell you, sir," I said.

"Jenkinson?" he clarified.

"Yes, sir," I acknowledged.

The deputy paused and said, "Then I'll tell you, and you'll say nothing. Then I'll make sure that Jenkinson hears that you said nothing."

I nodded in agreement.

"Jenkinson took the sword from the van. He took it across the fields and hid it somewhere," he continued. "Then he told you and Pratt that he had put it back on the van. Only speak if I have said something you disagree with."

I said nothing and the ordeal was over. Jenkinson was expelled, convinced that Barry and I had said nothing that would warrant a fork in the neck.

Chapter 16: Doodle – the Wonder Cat

February fell and my parents dream looked like it was on. We had been packing fastidiously, ready for our climb up the social ladder. Unfortunately, two days before the move, it became important to dad that his sons turned up well-groomed.

"Don't want the new neighbours thinking we have girls," dad said. It was a common ploy of the older generation to pretend they could not tell the difference between a girl and a boy with long hair.

"They could always look at our tits!" insisted Andrew, facetiously. It was not like him to resort to sarcasm or crudity. I was the one with the reputation of having an awkward streak, where my mouth tended to pre-empt my brain and it was refreshing to see my big brother leading a rebellion. However, our longer haired image was close to his heart.

"In the car, now!" was dad's response, glaring at all three of us.

"Thanks a lot, Andrew," I groaned, as the car sped toward the nearest barber shop.

"Thanks a lot, Andrew," echoed my six-year-old little brother. Sarcasm certainly sounded wrong coming from him.

"Well, we all know Eric doesn't want to be called a girl, don't we?" I retaliated uncharacteristically, remembering the park incident the previous summer.

We were all sensitive about wanting to have modern long hair. Our hair had started to creep down past our collars, in tribute to our idols. Mum was always the one to take us to the hairdressers and she was always careful to explain that we wanted to keep our ears covered, or at least a bit of longer hair hanging in front of the ear. We called these sideburns, even though the barber-shop manual technically saw sideburns as facial hair. Stevie Marriott of the Small Faces was my idol and the epitome of what a mod should look like.

Dad did not really have the sensitivity of mum, when explaining how he wanted our hair cut. In fact, he seemed to have the sympathy of the old-fashioned barber that he had chosen for our execution.

Dad had his usual, short-back-and-sides, to set the tone then it was Andrew's turn in the chair.

"Just half-an-inch off, please," Andrew instructed, "and can you leave my sideburns the way they are now."

The barber looked over at dad, for the real instructions, who shrugged and said, "Just make 'em look like boys."

This was like the green light to the barber to thumb his nose at modern trends. "You've got no sideburns," he replied, instantly snipping off the hair in front of his ears.

Next, he switched on his electric shaver and proceeded to buzz and snip until Andrew looked like Elvis Presley. I watched my brother turn pale and my empathy rose as he sat there speechless.

Then he was whisked out of the chair and it was my turn.

"I know I don't have sideburns but I want to keep the hair hanging in front of my ears the same as it is now," I told him. I did not want him making the same mistake that he had made on my brother.

"You don't have any sideburns," he repeated, as if it was his catchphrase and he had deliberately ignored my every word. I too got an Elvis special. I was devastated.

Englebert Humperdinck, on the barber's radio, did not help matters when he started to sing,

"There goes my reason for living, there goes my everything."

By the time, Eric got in the chair, Andrew and I sat seething in the waiting area. Dad was starting to realize the depth of despair that we were suffering and he suddenly saved Eric with a comment, not too short for this one. So, Eric, the five-year-old managed to escape with sideburns while my brother and I felt like we had been turned into something from the 1950's.

Luckily, it was half term, and we had a whole week off school, to grow our hair back.

Doodle was a spectacular tom cat. He had so many tricks up his sleeve and he had a different but special relationship with each member of the family. He had known Eric since the day he was born, so he still saw him as a baby, whom you must keep your claws permanently retracted around. Eric had pulled his tale, and poked him beyond provocation hundreds of times and Doodle simply tolerated it. Andrew loved to teach Doodle tricks. One time he made some miniature goal posts and invented a game where Doodle was the goalkeeper and he would flick milk-bottle tops at Doodle. At first, he was just teaching the cat to dive for the tops but soon he started to really try and score, only to discover that Doodle was deliberately protecting the goal and parrying away every attempt. Doodle loved this trick.

He also liked to climb out of upstairs open windows and sit on the window ledge. He would fall asleep fearlessly, out on the high ledge. On a couple of occasions, the window had ended up getting closed without us noticing he was out there. We would be searching all over, trying to track down where the meows were coming from. Nobody would ever admit who had closed the window but because of my legendary awkward streak, I was always the prime suspect.

Mum usually fed Doodle, and she could always get him in. He was a pretty fussy eater and would not touch Kit-I-Kat or any of the cheaper cat foods. He only liked the most expensive food, called 'Whiskers.' Usually the sound of the tin opening would bring him from half-a-mile away especially if accompanied by the high-pitched cry, "Doodle, Doodle, Doodle, Doodle, Doodle." Ironically, any member of the family could instinctively impersonate mum's five-word cry when needs be. Doodle was also fussy about the milk that he drank. He would only drink sterilized milk, which was commonly called 'dirty people's milk.' This version of nature's elixir never seemed to 'go off,' so people without refrigerators, who were presumably dirtier than fridge owners, acquired a similar taste to that of our cat.

Doodle had been brought home by dad as a kitten one day and it was him that named the cat. He had always had a Doodle in his family. Officially, this would have been Doodle Five, but to all of us he was number one. He was always bringing us presents; shrews were his favourites. Almost every day he would bring a shrew in the house, and play 'cat-and-mouse' with it. As a special treat, he would put the freshly killed prey in our shoes. Every one of us had experienced the grotesque feeling of slipping a foot into a shoe only to discover that it was competing for space with a half-dead rodent. He was pretty good at catching birds too, but he tended to leave a tell-tale trail of feathers, so they never came with the same shock.

Doodle always slept in my bed with me, so I felt like we had the closest relationship of all. On cold nights, he would climb under the covers and it was only his motorbike level purring that revealed his presence. There were a few occasions when he had been asleep, when mum had made my bed using a nursing trick aptly named 'hospital style,' where he ended up trapped under the excruciatingly tight sheets. Doodle loved to follow me around the garden, or into the fields, or often climb out on my window ledge. More and more frequently, I was finding him mysteriously locked out on the ledge of Eric's and my shared bedroom. I knew that I had not locked him out there and so I was beginning to fear that my little brother was playing a cruel trick on the cat. It was a little concerning because he denied it, however much I tried to trick him into confessing.

Then, on the day before the removal van was due to arrive Andrew and I were keeping out of the way. We were both still sulking about our extreme haircuts but moreover, we instinctively knew that packing would lead to frayed tempers and it was wise to remain sparse.

So, we were standing in the front garden, mentally saying, "Farewell" to the street where we'd lived since 1958. That's when we witnessed a true phenomenon, that had to be seen to be believed. Doodle suddenly darted, almost head on, at the front of the house and literally ran up the wall, in three or four bounds, settling on the upstairs sill of my window. Andrew and I were astonished and then we both turned to one another and spoke in unison.

"Did you see that?" We asked each other. We were both pleased to have a witness because it was one of those events that you could not report without feeling that the audience did not believe you. But it was true. Doodle had taught himself to run up the wall and settle casually on my bedroom windowsill.

We decided that, on removal day, we would have to keep a close eye on Doodle. In fact, mum borrowed a cat collar and leash off Kath Lockett, her friend and hairdresser. I was charged with making sure that Doodle made the transition successfully because, apparently, cats tended to be more attached to places than people. That was normal cats. Surely not our dirty-people-milk-drinking-shrew-taming-wall-climbing super-cat. He was Doodle, the people's cat.

The move went without a hitch really and we did not have too much to take with us, because dad had purchased most of the furniture of the family that we were succeeding. The weather was sunny, the new neighbours greeted us with open arms, it was probably refreshing for them to see such well-groomed teenagers, not looking a bit like girls. That was the first and last time they would see us without sideburns, that was for sure.

We had the finest view in Staffordshire. You could see Stoke City's football ground. In fact, you could see Stoke, Fenton, Longton and Trentham all from the lounge window. You could walk to the village of Penkville in ten minutes, dad's work was a twenty- minute walk away. We had a basement with a music room, a table tennis room, and an indoor garage. We had the most magnificent landscape garden in the city. Doodle found that his new paradise was even better than his old abode.

Chapter 16: Mary, Mary Quite Contrary

I was gaining a reputation of being a pretty cool First Year, with a popular, trendy brother, the smoking and the actively-embellished rumours of girl-snogging at the Top Rank and the move to a fancy house in the fancy part of town. Then that all turned head-over-heels, due to a freak moment of overconfidence, whilst interacting with the class nebbish.

Ewan Marston was probably the second most detested person in our class, preferred only to Tattersfield. He was small, with thick black wavy hair and even thicker black-rimmed spectacles, with the thickest lenses we had ever seen. They magnified his eyes giving him the look of a mad scientist. that made me suspect that even his parents mustn't have liked him. We somehow bastardized the name Marston into Mary, which enraged him every time he heard it. If only he could have resisted responding, the name would have died a natural death; after my scare with Tattersfield when he had attempted to christen me "Twink," I had a slight empathy for Mary's predicament. While we were waiting in line for PE class, Darren Trainor cracked a brilliant joke.

"Mary, you must have bloody good eyesight to see through those buggers," Darren commented on his goggles. It was hilarious.

Trainor was a puny red-haired boy himself, who would have probably been bully-fodder if he was not the master of quick wit. Marston seemed to be in no mood to be an object of ridicule and he turned beet red. Suddenly, he charged at Trainor with his arms wind-milling. Not for the first time in my life, I stepped in to protect my best friend. I was no tough guy but a swinging Mary would surely desist when he saw how easily I could 'make a monkey' of him, with my agility and athleticism. Indeed, the line cheered as I sidestepped the onslaught of flailing limbs. I even had chance to take an arrogant head-nod to acknowledge my peers' laughter.

The sounds rose to crescendo. In fact, the audience became so excitable, watching the wafting clownery, I was suddenly aware that the noise might draw Fizzer out of his room, and he would be so antagonized that he might end up making us do an hour of circuit training. This distracting thought left me with my guard down and out-of-the-blue, Mary's cupped hand caught my ear full-on, forcing a whoosh of compressed air down my external canal.

It was instantly silent.

I was suddenly deaf in my right ear and, at that exact same moment, Fizzer Westwood stepped out of his office to check the commotion. He signalled for us to file into the changing rooms without a sound. In less than a minute we were sitting on the hard gym floor in our white T-shirts, matching short and socks and freshly whitened plimsolls, awaiting inspection.

In terror, I must have turned as white as our PE kits because the eternally-angry Fizzer seemed to muster-up some compassion.

"What the fizzing heck's wrong with you, Wells?" His distant voice filtered into my right ear.

"Nothing sir," I responded, shocked by the extent of my sudden disability. Squealing to the teachers, even on the despicable Mary, just was not an option.

"Come with me," he ordered, taking me into the mini gym staff room where no child had ever been.

"What's wrong with you, Wells? His muffled voice asked again, "you're pale as a ghost!"

"I can't hear, sir!" I explained in my panic.

Fizzer looked confused. He shouted even louder, "You're as pale as a ghost!"

"I've gone deaf, sir!" I responded. It felt like I was shouting but the lack of sound in my left ear was quite eerie.

I thought for a second that he was going to repeat it again but then his puzzlement turned to understanding and that's when my tears started to flow. Fizzer turned human briefly and he marched me to the secretary in the school office, who called my dad at work. Thirty minutes later, my mum and dad turned up and drove me straight to the hospital, still in my PE outfit, clutching my uniform, wrapped up in my blazer.

Dad pulled a few strings, then delivered me and mum to the waiting room of Mr. Fitzpatrick, the Ears Nose and Throat (ENT) specialist. Apparently, when you rose to the ranks of consultant then the title Doctor was replaced by the term Mister. It sounded more like a demotion to me.

"Watch yourself with Dr Flirtypants," dad teased mum. She loved it when he acted jealous.

"Actually, it's Mr Flirtypants," she responded, giving him nothing to allay his green-eyed monster. Mum always went into a peculiar mood whenever she took us to the doctors. As a nurse herself, she was of the opinion that the nurses did all of the work and the doctors took all the glory. She viewed consultants as being a step further removed from reality. Under the circumstances, I chose to hope that Mr Fitzpatrick at least knew one end of the otoscope from the other.

It was odd because, even though I had only damaged my left ear, 'Righty' seemed to have shut down in some gesture of solidarity with his twin. So, when mum kept firing questions at me, it was like watching a silent movie. It was nice to meet a nurse who grasped the fact that ENT patients needed you to talk slowly and succinctly. She took me in a very technically sophisticated room.

"I'm going to do a few tests, do you understand?" she over-articulated, placing some headphones on my ears.

I nodded a positive response.

"I want you to give me the 'thumbs up' sign whenever you hear a sound," she told me.

I nodded again. Then gave the 'thumbs up' sign, to demonstrate that I knew my mission.

First I started to hear some bleepy, followed by trumpy noises in my right ear. I was thumbs-upping every couple of seconds. Then she seemed to be having mechanical difficulties with the machine, as I waited patiently for the next part of the experiment. She was apparently playing the bleeps and farts in my left ear but to no avail. She looked concerned, rushed out to talk to my mum. She came back in again, removed the headphones and placed a tube in my ear and began to pump air. It was the strangest sensation because I could taste cool air in the back of my throat. Apparently, this was proof that my eardrum was perforated because

179

air was managing to get down my eustachian tube, but it would take a consultant to confirm this obvious conclusion. The nurse made some notes and then began to mime to me that I was a 'brave young man.' That felt like a precursor to some really bad news because I had been anything but brave.

After an eternal wait I finally got to meet the handsome, alleged womanizer, Mr Fitzpatrick. His studious avoidance of eye-contact, seemed to suggest that I would be walking out with a gruesome flesh-coloured hearing aide.

He poked his otometer in my right ear and started by declaring the good news, "Well this one's fine!" Sure enough, as if reassurance was all it needed, 'Righty' jumped straight back to full function.

"I'm not having a hearing aid!" I protested.

He still did not look at me, directly. Instead, he focused all his attention on my mum. If mum held contempt for his station, she certainly kept it hidden. In fact, his deep voice seemed to trigger an involuntary lip-pouting gesture every time he said a word. Mr Fitzpatrick reeked of self-assurance. He swivelled me around and tugged at my left ear until it was manoeuvred onto the otoscope.

He started with the bad-news-preamble, "You're a brave young man," which I read to mean, *"You are about to hear some dreadful news and I want you to be brave about it!"*

He turned to mum and smiled a seductive smile saying, "You know, if you put glasses on him he'd look just like Peter." He might not have thought me important enough to make eye-contact but his film-star stare seemed to have a tractor-beam lock on mum's big brown eyes. Amidst my lowest point in life, they seemed to be having a flirty moment.

For a split second, my displaced thought patterns flashed back to the dreaded clinic glasses that had plagued my earlier years. High school life would not have been worth living if I had still had that particular cross to bear. A sadistic optician had even made me have sticking plaster over my lazy eye for a time which was the cruellest torture of all. Of course, this was Mary's situation; it was his 'Freddy and the Dreamers' glasses that made his every waking moment unbearable. Now, I would be in direct competition with him, for the honour of being class gimp, once they had fitted me with a pink-flesh coloured hearing aide.

"Is there permanent damage?" Mum asked, refocusing the lascivious doctor. He seemed as diverted as me.

"Errrrr. Permanent?........ Permanent?" He was refocusing his brain. "No, his hearing will come back."

"Really?" Mum asked.

"When?" I interrupted.

"Oh, maybe a day or two, or a week, depends on his healing power."

I could not believe how casual his voice was, as he delivered the most important news of my life. Any animosity dissolved and was replaced with elation. Suddenly, I could have hugged Doctor Flirtypants myself, or should I say Mr. Flirtypants? I suspect that he wanted to hug my mum. She kissed my cheek with delight, leaving a deposit of red lipstick that had magically appeared on my mum's lips from nowhere.

Sure enough, the next morning I awakened and, by the grace of God, I could hear again. All of a sudden, I begun to appreciate music, which cemented itself as my favourite stimulus. I switched on the radio, and it happened to be my favourite band, The Move singing, "I Can Hear the Grass Grow." It could easily instead have been Thor's unfavourite, "The Sound of Silence."

Chapter 17: The Ash Tree

Just outside the bottom of the garden was a fifty-foot sycamore tree. The first branch was seven feet from the ground. In other words, a simple leap and backward somersault would have you balancing on your stomach. Then the next 30 feet offered a ladder of branches, up through the lush camouflage of leaves. In fact, with my acrobatic agility, I mastered the art of leaping from the garden wall and rotating to instantaneous invisibility. Eric was the first to witness the trick and he was agog, believing I had magically gone. It was fun to be able to disappear in a flash but more useful was that the leaves served as a one-way mirror, so that we could hide and observe everything that happened in the house and garden.

Our new garage was like an Aladdin's Cave, full of discarded wooden shelves and rusty tools. In no time, we were sawing and nailing and building secluded platforms up our tree, as well as a few strategically place six-inch nails to aid the climb. Andrew got new batteries for a discarded transistor radio, and built it its own ledge. It got better reception up the tree than it did on the ground. Drew laughed when he switched it on and the song playing was Eddie Floyd singing, "Knock on wood!" This serendipity was beyond amusement to me.

He nailed an empty tobacco tin to the branch, to the beat of the song. This was to serve as an ashtray. Then he pulled an African jewellery box out of his jacket, to stash cigarettes and matches. It became our joke that we called it the Ash tree, and everyone always corrected us that it was a Sycamore. In no time, we had our secret hide-away. We could watch dad twenty feet below us, mowing the lawn, while we blatantly blew smoke rings and Jimi Hendrix sang about Purple Haze.

Other than the relative palatial nature of our new house, the Plusogram, as dad called it, was the greatest addition to our life. All of my friends were constantly buying 45's to play on their monophonic record players. Now we had a stereogram, our new raison d'etre. It made birthday's easy to buy for too.

March was birthday month in the Wells household. Andrew got Sergeant Pepper's Lonely Hearts Club Band, probably still the greatest album ever recorded. Unfortunately, I bought him the stereo version, which turned out to be 'not a patch' on the mono mix. Still, it had been at the top of the album charts for a year, since knocking off the Sound of Music soundtrack. Mum got Something Stupid, a duet between Frank and Nancy Sinatra. I got a record called Paper Sun by a band called Traffic. It was the first band I had heard of that were so cool that they didn't even have the word "The" before their title.

My dad was so proud to have joined the realms of landed gentry, he had not really had any interest in gardening but now that he was the 'owner' of a magnificent landscape he intended to keep it immaculate. Mum was also loving her elevated station in life.

"We should have a house-warming party! Mum declared.

Dad's face lit up initially but then he frowned as a mental image of Nana Lena saying snobbish things to his friends brought him down to Earth.

"Better not, Bet," he responded.

"It's your mother, isn't it?" Mum asked, showing more intuition than usual.

He nodded in agreement, "She'd be unbearable. She'd be telling everybody how she had given you a thousand pounds for the deposit."

"I know," mum empathized, "she would not be able to stop herself."

"And she'd be drinking champers and going all snobby around my colleagues. I couldn't bear it, Beryl."

"Well it was a nice thought," she acquiesced.

Andrew, who loved the idea of a party, was not willing to let it drop so easily. He asked, "Why would an old person want to come to a groovy party?" It was the perfect pitch to resurrect the dying subject.

"Yes, she won't want to be dancing to loud music on the Plusogram," I added, my mockery going unrecognized.

"He's right Peter, maybe she wouldn't even want to come," said mum

"Oh, she'd not want to miss an opportunity to tell all my friends that she technically 'owns' the house. I'm surprised she hasn't already taken out a bloody announcement in The Evening Sentinel," he explained, visibly shuddering at the thought.

It was now my job to push the case.

"Nana Lena doesn't have to ever know about the party," I said, "and if she finds out you could just apologize, saying that it never occurred to you that she would be interested in a groovy young people's party."

Andrew, mum and Eric all agreed with my logic and waited, in anticipation of dad's response.

His expression changed from puzzlement to devilment, as he declared, "Sod it, let's have a party!"

"Yes!" We all cheered in one voice.

"But we must keep it secret from my mother," he qualified.

"Mum's the word," I joked.

"Mum's definitely not the word!" he replied, tickled more by my response than to my brilliant joke.

In a way, this was the first ever democratic family decision that I had ever known, in that we had all chipped in with persuasive arguments and ended up with a solution that suited everyone.

Andrew had been studying democracy in school and he was always trying to clarify his thoughts by explaining things to me. Apparently, the haircut decision, a month earlier, was an example of a total dictatorship. Andrew had always been the diplomat of the family but he was becoming a little more rebellious, since hitting his teens. In this instant, I felt that Andrew's cleverness lay in appealing to the youthfulness of my parents. Using the word 'groovy' seemed to draw the generation line, even though it was not an expression that they would normally use.

Our household had never had so much as a birthday bash, so a fully-fledged grown-up, house-warming party was out of our realm of expertise. Suddenly, my parents were renting a cut-glass punch bowl with matching glasses and mum was learning recipes for flaky pastry delicacies and open-top baps. They were buying coasters and doilies, and debating whether paper plates were unsophisticated.

They wanted us to wear our school shirts and trousers and act as serving hosts. However, a last-minute negotiation brought an eleventh-hour reprieve so that we could wear our Top Rank hipsters and ultra-modern crew-neck sweaters. The party was scheduled to start at 9pm but the only ones to arrive on time were the neighbours. The Biltons next door, misjudged the sophistication level, and turned up clutching a home-baked Quiche Lorraine and a bottle of German Liebfraumilch wine. The Carter's from the other side, who turned up simultaneously, seemed embarrassed at arriving empty-handed. Dad had the diplomatic task of trying to assure the Biltons that their offering was perfect, at the same time as reassuring the Carter's that they were not expected to bring anything.

Mr. Gault, from down the road, left his downtrodden wife at home. He had a London accent and an air of confidence that had apparently come from years of being in sales. Apparently, he had a reputation of being a bit of a 'ladies' man, even though he was married with children.

"He's not my type but I can see his appeal," mum commented, with some ambiguity.

"He's a chinless wonder," dad responded, with no ambiguity.

"Would you like to try the punch?" Andrew offered, just as mum had trained him. The punch was a brandy-based drink with Cointreau, Martini, lemonade and orange juice. There were also slices of orange and lemon floating around in it. Andrew was keen to use the ladle that came with the punch-bowl.

"I'll have a glass of Liebfraumilch," Mr Bilton responded, turning and glaring at his wife.

"Liebfraumilch for me, too," came her delayed response. She was obviously contemplating the punch but the Biltons felt obliged to recoup what they'd brought.

Eric was sent in at this point with a platter of little sausages on sticks, while I followed in relay, with a plate of cheese and pineapple cubes sharing the same cocktail sticks. Eric and I had been responsible for their construction earlier, so we were interested to monitor their popularity.

'Chinless' Gault, took the sausage and cheese nibbles as well as scooping himself a glass of punch, by-passing the ladle, much to Andrew's annoyance.

Ted and Bertha arrived next, and the place suddenly sounded like a party. I took everyone's coats and lay them on mum and dad's beds as instructed. Then, I was sent on another cocktail sausage run, while Eric took over the pineapple surprises, as we had cleverly nicknamed them.

"You've got the hardest job," Bertha flattered Andrew, as he carefully ladled out punch for my parent's closest friends. But then Chinless swooped in, scooped his glass in for a second drink, as if to demonstrate the simplicity of his job. Furthermore, he then used his fingers to chase a piece of lemon around the bowl a couple of times before fishing it out to garnish his drink. This seemed to inspire him to launch into a joke.

"So, this nun goes to the Mother Superior and says, "I think I'm pregnant, what shall I do?"

The Mother Superior replied, "You could try sucking a lemon."

"Will that stop me being pregnant?" the nun asked.

"No but it'll help wipe that smile off your face!" Exclaimed the Mother Superior.

Chinless Gault led the audience laughter, which could, at best be described as polite. Ted, who would normally laugh raucously at anything my dad said, made a point of keeping his response to a subdued chuckle. Bertha obviously found the bawdy joke funny but she checked herself quickly when she remembered that there were children in the room.

On the other hand, the grown-ups were starting to let their guards down. Suddenly there was an influx of people. I was developing a scientific theory about the relationship between arrival time and boringness, when it came to adult parties. Even the coats of the second round of guests seemed more eccentric, as Eric and I spent the next half-an-hour traipsing up to the makeshift cloakroom.

Andrew's expertise at punch distribution evolved as he manned the ladle. Initially, very precise proportions of each fluid were used to mix the elixir. However, Andrew replenished with increasing randomness, favouring the alcohol to the soft drink dilutions.

I had an old Egmond guitar, with F holes, that I had bought from Rosina Ward's pawn shop in Hanley, but I had never even managed to get it in tune. I had mastered "Pictures of Matchstick men" by Status Quo on the first string but didn't think that my guitar would ever offer more than that. But two punch-drunk nurses grabbed the guitar and after a couple of twiddles on the machine heads, one was blasting out the most melodious versions of a song called "Railroad Bill." The other added sublime harmonies and the whole party was transfixed. I was instantly infatuated with these two nurses but what I really fell in love with was my own guitar. Their version of "Sloop John B" absolutely clinched it for me; I wanted to be a guitarist.

After a few more rounds of sausage rolls, brandy snaps filled with whipped cream, not to mention Mrs Bilton's quiche, Eric and I sat down to do a bit of people-watching. Chinless Gault was a study all on his own. I realized that, unlike myself, his 'success with the ladies' relied entirely on two distinct factors. Firstly, he had no fear of rejection. Some of the younger nurses would laugh openly in his face, in response to his bawdy jokes and increasingly lascivious comments. But he remained noticeably unphased. The second feature was his ability to play the numbers game. Nine out of ten rejections would have destroyed me at the Top Rank, but Chinless saw it as a one in ten success rate. Sure enough, a matron, with a matronly figure finally acquiesced to his advances and it was not long before she was sharing one of her numerous chins with him, with a serious snogging session in the entrance hall. It was not a pretty sight. I would have stopped watching sooner if it was not for the fascination. However, I did make a mental note of his principles, all be them adulterous, which I detested.

The alcohol was starting to have an influence on the party. Everybody appeared to find everything hilarious.

"Would anyone care for a sausage?" I announced to the living room.

"That's my job!" a junior doctor responded. Raucous laughter from an entourage of nurses ensued. Andrew had to explain to me that this doctor worked at the Clinic for Venereal Disease, so he was within his rights to claim to "care for sausage." I chuckled retrospectively and then I cringed with embarrassment to think that the nurses may have thought that I was trying to be crude.

It was hard to work out how much of the party atmosphere was due to the punch. But the crowd's ebullience was infectious. Soon, our family were the only sober people at the party. That didn't last long.

Mum finally relaxed enough say, "I think I'll try a glass of punch myself." She never drank more than two Babychams normally and dad had always commented that she would be drunk 'at the sniff of a barmaid's apron.' The punch worked quickly because her last ironic words of sanity for the evening were, "I don't think there's any alcohol in this." Next thing she was chasing Doodle around the house, trying to show how agreeable he was. Doodle certainly did not agree and he had enough sense to keep running, much to everyone's amusement.

Seeing mum lose control seemed to empower my elder brother to experiment with the magic punch, himself. He looked at me and, with a finger to his lips to forge a bond of secrecy, he proceeded to ladle out a full glass and knock it back. I saw him shudder, then he beckoned me over with the ladle but I shook my head. If inebriation hit mum fast, then Andrew quickly took over the record for that. I could see that he was already struggling to manipulate the ladle and he resorted to the Chinless Gault approach to glass filling. He did not shudder as much with the second glass full. But this was probably because his senses were already becoming anaesthetized. Andrew abandoned his bar duties and set off to help mum corner the cat.

"He's going to break a few girls' hearts," a nurse told mum.

"Ooooh Beryl, if I was five years younger," one of the nurses said to mum.

The party was in full swing when the phone rang. There had been several calls earlier in the evening, from wastrels who had mislaid the address but somehow retained the phone number. The early calls had caused mum to shush the crowd as she answered, just in case it was the dreaded Nana Lena. However, she rarely called after nine thirty so this ring did not create cause for alarm. Even if it was, mum's pursuit of the 'genius' cat had her totally pre-occupied.

Andrew picked up the phone, but he was too inebriated to chant out the normal greeting.

"Hello, this is Lena, is that Peter?" asked Nana Lena. "What's all that noise?"

"Errr…..errr" responded the stunned Andrew. He was not sure what to say. But worst still, he started to giggle uncontrollably.

"Who is that? Get me Peter!" she demanded.

My dad was the first to twig that there was something wrong, as he moved toward the hallway where the phone was situated. He tried to quieten the partiers in the hallway, with a palms-to-the-ground damping down gesture, which eventually caught on, and the hushed lull spread around the room. The only sound was Andrew trying desperately to choke his laughter.

Dad shrugged at him as if to say, "Who is it?"

Andrew did not know how to respond, so he made a fire-coming-from-the-mouth gesture, which presumably was his interpretation of a dragon. This seemed to tickle him further and he almost yelped trying to hold back his hysteria. Mum joined the hallway at this point and she instantly sobered up at the prospect of her worst nightmare. She tried to grab the phone out of Andrew's hand but he indicated that he had the situation in hand.

"Peter, Peter, is that you? The whole audience heard. "It sounds like there's a party going on. Are you having a party?"

Mum again tried and failed to retrieve the phone from her drunken son.

Then Andrew responded, "Harro, Chinese Take-away, can I have you order preeese?" he said in a deadpan voice.

"Who's this?" said Lena's voice.

"This Hoo Flung Dung, who this?" he said.

"I think I might have the wrong number," said Lena, to pin-drop silence.

"Solly, long number!" said Andrew, putting down the phone. The crowd went wild. It was hilarious.

Mum was conflicted between relief and embarrassment of her son's state. "Come here, Mister Hoo Flung Dung." Andrew took off down the stairs toward the basement at a faster rate than Doodle had previously managed. Mum did not dare chase him, as her new duty was to guard the phone, anticipating that an irate Nana Lena would be calling straight back. Her encounter with Mister Flung Dung had discombobulated my grandmother, leaving her with no desire for any more out-of-whack conversations. It was hard to say how mum would have responded if the phone had rung again.

Andrew raced downstairs, continued out through the garage door and into the floodlit garden, where as the hard liquor continued to surge through his veins. It was nice to see my brother be the naughty one, although I did not enjoy him taking over the mantle of being the 'funny one.' I was tempted to sample the ladle myself but I instinctively felt that somebody in the family, other than Eric, needed to remain sober.

Chapter 19: Whacky Races

One day, Boothroyd sent me to the school office to get a form list. The office lady gave me a couple, so I decided to keep one for myself. I overheard Adams and Bentley talking about a Cartoon on television, called Whacky Races. Of course, I was far too sophisticated to acknowledge its existence, but I had secretly watched it. With the form list in my hand, a brilliant scheme hatched in my mind: Whacky Races betting pool. So, I set the odds based on several factors and took the bets.

Dick Dastardly and his dog Mutley, never won - the basic theme of the race was Dastardly's effort to sabotage everyone else! It was amazing how my odds of 33-1 attracted the punters. Chris Gotham went without lunch for the day to put a shilling on them. Penelope Pitstop and Peter Perfect had each won twice recently, so I was confident to give them both longer odds of 6-1. I was convinced that the Anthill Mob or the Arkansas Chugabug were the most likely winners so they were offered at 2-1. My pockets were jingling with silver coins, as I sped home to catch the race. I had sixteen shillings and I was mightily relieved when the Anthill mob pipped Dastardly and Mutley to the finish line.

After paying out two shillings I realized what a good scheme I had going.

Then next week, I made over a quid, as the bets came flooding in. I would have owed fifty if Dastardly had not kept stopping to set traps for others. Amazingly, Penelope Pitstop, the southern belle, won her third race in 5 weeks. Mary and Tattersfield both took money off me from that bet working entirely on pervy cartoon crushes, rather than logic. I still made a healthy profit, netting two pounds, which I instantly spent at Cadman's music shop on a record.

I bought "The Who Sell Out," which turned out to be one of the finest albums ever made. It was one of the first concept albums, where all the songs were linked with adverts and pirate radio. Even the cover was hilarious, with Roger Daltrey sitting in a bathful of sticky baked beans, and John Entwistle, the normally introvert bass-player, dressed as a puny muscle-man with a voluptuous woman at his side. I played the album over and over, until I knew every song and sound intimately.

Every school has a miscellaneous worker, with a false sense of authority, perpetually frustrated by the 'rudeness of children today.' They feel that the teachers are not tough enough and they end up in unnecessary petty squabbles with students. It may be the caretaker, or a dinner lady, or office staff. At Hartley, High school it was the technician, Woolbridge.

Woolbridge was an obese, ruddy cheeked man, undoubtedly with some blood pressure issues. He wore clinic glasses and sported a greased, short-back-and-sides haircut. It was his use of Brylcream that inspired Darren Trainor to nickname him, "Fire-risk Woolbridge," which was not an ideal handle for someone working all day in a chemistry lab. Some kids called him Woolly Bully, after a song, based on a dance.

'Fire-risk' drove a rusty red Austin A35, which was hardly big enough to accommodate his massive frame. Unlike, most staff, who used the staff carpark, Woolbridge would insist on manoeuvring to the back of the school, to have his junk heap near to the science labs. His day started badly every single morning as he frantically honked his horn to make the passive aggressive kids, gathered on smoker's corner, move out of the way. One day, he seriously lost his patience and he ploughed manically into a scattering crowd, as smoky-lunged youth leapt for their lives.

As much as he hated Children, Woolly Bully worshipped Downing, the biology teacher. He hardly spoke a sentence that didn't start with 'Mr Downing.' For all his strengths as a teacher, Downing would often keep the class waiting outside his room, as he squeezed in an extra cigarette in the back prep room. On one occasion, he sent Mr Woolbridge out to 'quieten the rabble' as we impatiently awaited our teacher.

"Mr Downing says that you rabble have to be quiet until he comes out." Insisted Woolly Bully. That sounded like a name Downing would use, but for some reason, our class was a little offended hearing it come from Woolbridge's lips.

"Rabble, rabble," chuntered Trainor under his breath. It caught on in a flash.

"Rabble, rabble, rabble," repeated thirty pupils, in very low decibels, in complete unison. It was like the soft hum of a motorboat, or perhaps an Australian Didgeridoo orchestra warming up.

"Stop that noise!" yelled Woolly but the group sensed that he could not really work out what was happening. Trainor was orchestrating the sound, which seemed to get louder or softer at the whim of the group. The group noise was almost like a religious experience, and I sensed why meditating monks enjoyed their mantras. As much as we were enjoying the mystical moment, Woolbridge was detesting it.

"I'll cane the lot of you, if you don't stop!" he insisted. This was an empty threat on two fronts – Firstly, mass caning was not allowed because, it would inevitably lay the school open to charges of indiscriminate punishment. Secondly, Woolbridge did not have the powers of *loco parentis* that teachers possessed. Teachers could beat children at will, if they could justify that it was a discipline that any 'reasonable parent' may carry out. However, even in the unlikelihood that a reasonable parent would want to beat his thirty children with a stick,

Woolly Bully would be subject to charges of 'assault on a minor,' if he tried it.

The droning went on, as did Woolbridge's babbling, "Well I won't cane you but Mr Downing will cane you."

That was a slightly more valid threat because Downing had an affection for Woolly Bully. It stopped half the rabble from 'rabbling,' leaving the rest of us feeling slightly less emboldened. Woolbridge, felt empowered by his partial success.

"And if you bring your parents up, I'll hit them as well," added the beetroot red technician.

"You wouldn't dare hit my dad!" Adams told him.

It finally went silent.

"Well, I won't hit him, Mr Downing will hit him," said Woolly. He was feeling proud that he had gained control of the rebel rabble and that he had achieved pin-drop quietness. However, then he visibly shivered as he heard a voice from behind him:

"What have you been planning for me, Mr Woolbridge?' he asked, with a wicked grin.

"Nothing Mr Downing," he responded adding another shade of crimson to his hue.

"You've got a boxing match with Adams's dad, sir," reported Whittle.

"Sorry sir," said Adams, knowing how Downing's perverse smile could often evolve into a sadistic punishment.

"Oh well Adams, tell your dad it's Queensbury Rules," smiled Downing.

"It's just a joke, sir," Adams replied. Adams had once been as cheeky as Whittle, but the Hardman's caning had permanently taken all the fun out of his personality.

"Nothing funny about the Queensbury Rules, Adams. The Marquees of Queensbury spent a long time drafting them." said Downing, winking at Woolbridge, as he spoke.

"Sorry, sir," said Adams, as a single teardrop rolled down his face. It seemed to appease Woolly Bully, as he interpreted Downing's sarcasm as personal support, and he stood nodding to himself. Downing sensed that he was touching on a raw nerve with Adams, and stopped right there. I remembered why he was my favourite teacher, in that moment. Unlike Boothroyd, he had humanity.

"Okay, game over, boys," he announced, which seemed to satisfy everyone. "File in silently, and get your books out."

We complied, without a further rumble, or 'rabble' for that matter.

Chapter 20: 'Scuse Me, While I Kiss the Sky

My brother, Andrew, went on a school trip to Austria that Easter. Unlike my Isle of Man experience, earlier in the year, high school field trips were very much under-regulated. The teacher chaperones did not have specific duties - they were on their own junkets. So, forty-five high school boys were let loose on the bier kellers of Salzburg.

Whilst he was away, I got the opportunity to make his life complete. It was announced that a concert tour was coming to Hanley Gaumont, with someone for everyone. Cat Stevens and Englebert

Humperdink would be touring with The Walker Brothers. However, the act that would make Andrew worship me forever was an upcoming guitar phenomenon called Jimi Hendrix. I lined up with hordes of screaming girls for over three hours, which was a life-changing experience. In fact, there was a picture of the queue on the Sentinel's front page the next day; I kept the newspaper for posterity, even though I was just out-of-shot. I paid six shillings each, for two tickets to the matinee performance.

I could hardly contain myself for the next week, anticipating the moment, when I could break the news. At first, I wanted to meet him at the coach, when dad picked him up but then I began to plan or more exquisite revelation.

I swear that Andrew seemed to have grown three inches, in the two weeks he had been away in Austria. Perhaps his deportment had changed but it was noticeable the second he climbed out of the car. School trips were legendary for producing defining moments of growth, and his 'presence' had definitely changed. It was like he was 'all business' as he insisted that dad pop the boot of the car and carried his own suitcase into the house. He walked with a slight John Wayne swagger which mum mistook for a limp.

"Have you hurt your leg?" she asked, as her mothering instinct kicked in.

"No, it's fine!" he tutted, showing an irritation that he would normally have been able to control.

"He's tired, Beryl. He's been traveling non-stop for thirty-six hours," dad excused him.

He let mum give him a quick hug and kiss but more like a reluctant teenager than the 'lost lamb' that mum was trying to welcome back into her fold.

"Let me look at that leg," insisted the nurse in mum.

He pulled away dramatically.

"No!" he suddenly yelled, "I said, it's fine!"

"Leave him, Bet," dad insisted. Dad seemed to have an empathy with my normally placid brother's rebellion.

Andrew popped the catches of his case and pulled out some presents.

Eric got a bright red Austrian hat, with a feather sticking out of it. He had cleverly packed the hat by creating a dent in his clothes, then filling the hat with socks and underwear, in a plastic bag.

"Wow!" Eric exclaimed with delight.

"It's a yodelling hat!" Andrew told our little brother.

Sure enough, as soon as he put it on, Eric began to yodel. It was funny for the first ten minutes but it wore thin as the night progressed.

Mum got a swiss clock in the shape of a swiss cabin and with a couple of bluebirds that rocked back and forth in unison, with a small dangling pendulum. It kept awful time but there was a tiny brass weight attached to the pendulum, which could be raised or lowered to adjust the tick rate. Everyone tried but nobody ever mastered the exact position. The only thing you could rely on, about that clock was that it would never ever show the correct time. Despite this, mum loved it because her angelic firstborn had spent his limited spending money on it. In reality, he had stolen it while a naive Austrian shop-keeper was distracted reaching down for the red hat.

Dad was next and he was not disappointed. He got a Perspex keyring with a real Edelweiss, the Austrian national flower made infamous by the song from The Sound of Music, sealed inside. You could not get that from Woolworths. He said that he had been wanting a keyring to put the house spare, which he now hung from a strategically placed nail behind the drainpipe at the back of the new house. I saw Andrew's face drop, as I am sure he expected it to replace the Sunbeam Rapier tag attached to dad's car key. I was bursting with anticipation as to what my gift would be, as well as bubbling with excitement about the revelation of the Hendrix tickets.

It fell silent as mum asked, "So what did you get for Mart?"

Andrew blushed, obviously caught off guard, before spluttering out, "Nothing."

Everyone gasped in unison.

"Andrew!" mum said in a 'we didn't raise you this way' tone.

"Well it hasn't arrived yet," he adjusted his answer.

My mind instantly went to the Manx kippers that I had shipped to dad earlier in the year. Surely, he had not sent me kippers because he knew that I detested them. Anyway, being surrounded by land, it was unlikely that Austria would have any significant fish industry. Maybe it was a special Austrian Knoptwurst - allegedly the finest sausage in the world. He glanced over to me and with the subtlest of eyerolls, he indicated that, whatever he had, it was not suitable for the parents to see. Maybe it was a pen with an image of a woman in a swimsuit, who magically became naked when you turned her upside down? Perhaps it was dirty playing cards? Whatever it was, if it had to be kept from parents, it must have been something exciting. I could hardly wait.

"I'm going to bed," he announced, still walking like a cowboy from the fifties movies.

"Andrew, there's something wrong with your leg dear." mum stated again. "Have you been bitten by any weird Austrian insects?"

"No mum my leg's fine!" he insisted.

"Goodnight, son," said dad, "glad to see you back."

"Yodel-ay-eat-ee!" said Eric.

"Take that yodelling fool with you," laughed dad.

"Yodel-ay-eat-ee!" said Eric.

One minute later Andrew was trying to suppress a scream, as his left shin suffered excruciating agony.

"Yodel-ay-ee-pigging-tee!" screamed Andrew, as all his leg hairs were being ripped out, as he removed the Sellotape that had been securing my present to his leg for thirty-six hours. A flick-knife!

My brother had hobbled through the Nothing-To-Declare section of customs, with deadly contraband taped to his leg. Now, I was the proud owner of an illegal weapon.

"Bet you've never seen one of those before?" he asked, trying to milk my gratitude. My mind jumped back to the moment that I thought I was holding Kenny Trotters dick but it turned out to be a flick-knife. However, I was not sure that I would be able to explain that, so I let it drop.

"No, never," I replied.

Unbelievably, it was the next day before I remembered the Hendrix tickets. This added to the web of revelation that I had in mind. Mum switched on the radio as we milked up our cereal, and sure enough Englebert Humperdink was singing "Please release me."

"Englebert's coming to Hartley in April, isn't he Mart?" mum prompted me.

"Not sure, mum," I responded with pseudo-disinterest.

"Kath Lockett loves Englebert Humperdink" mum added, "Personally, I can't bear his fat lips!"

It was hard to tell if Andrew was paying attention but he must have been hearing this.

"He's on with The Walker Brothers, I think," I told her.

Andrew's ears picked up then.

"Oh, that's right," mum added. "I read it in The Sentinel. They sold out in record time. Look." she said, placing the copy of the local newspaper on the table in front of him, with the sell-out article on full display.

As I reached for the newspaper, my brother grabbed it and started to read the article. I saw his eyes widen as he read that Cat Stevens and his new hero, Jimi Hendrix were also on the bill.

"Bloody Hell!" screamed my brother, "Hendrix is playing."

"Whose Hendrix?" mum played along.

"Bloody Hell. He's only the world's greatest guitarist! Bloody Hell!" he groaned. You could hear his voice tone drop as the elation that his hero was coming to town turned to despair at the concert being 'sold out.'

The initial plan was to drag it out for longer but I could not wait any longer.

"I got us both tickets." I stated coldly.

He looked perplexed.

"I got us tickets." I said again, placing the two tickets in front of him.

Now his eyes were as wide as saucers.

"Mart, I could kiss you!" he said.

"You'd better not!" I laughed.

"Oh, I bet Kath Lockett would like those," laughed mum, pretending to grab at them.

"No bloody way!" my brother and I said in unison.

After the Easter holidays, it was actually fun to go back to school. Bragging to the friends that we were going to a Hendrix concert and showing off my illegal flick knife made me feel like I had arrived. I also started to hear stories about my perfect brothers far-from-perfect antics on his Austrian trip.

It seems that he had spent most of his week in bier kellers, smoking, drinking and chasing the fraulines. In fact, his drunken condom-inflating escapade, which allegedly got him kicked-out of a bar, was the talk of the school. He apparently blew up three lubricated rubber Johnnies and he and his four peers played a game called "catch the greased pig,' before the bier keller owner kicked them out. He was also reputed to have enjoyed a particularly advanced petting session with a frauline, but the more I inquired into this, the more incredulous his story became; I was desperate for details but his tale seemed to change every time I asked him to elaborate. I concluded that his frauline was mainly fictitious.

Unlike the Isle of Man, which was heavily regulated to the point of forcing us to wear Stanley

210

Matthews shorts and jankers-reinforced curfews, high school trips were notoriously unsupervised. Being stuck on a coach for a couple of days with excitable, sex starved teenage boys, was considered more than penance for the 'free' holiday that the free-loading teachers, and partners needed to tolerate. Austrian bar owners seemed to operate on the assumption that children were self-regulating, when it came to alcohol consumption. So, Andrew, unperturbed by the post house-warming party hangover, embarked on an apparent week of debauchery. Some real and some fabricated. So, the perfect child, as mum would describe his early years, was starting to flourish, as he experimented with the less mundane aspects of growing up. Tales of drunken prophylactic inflating episodes, obnoxious taunts of the Salzburg locals and premeditated shoplifting sprees filled me with shame and adulation, in equal measure.

Having learned from The Move concert earlier in the year, I opted for the matinee performance. It seemed the bands were on a challenging tour, driving from one city to the next, overnight, working the afternoon audience into a frenzy, decompressing for an hour and then starting again with an even more frenetic evening show. The Beatles had set a new set of rules for audiences. Basically, girls screamed at the top of their lungs from start to finish. They fed off each other's hysteria and fainting was considered a definite 'feather in the cap' of any serious fan and some girls worked full throttle to achieve this state of nirvana.

Our seats were half way down this relatively small venue and Andrew approved of my selection. We had a perfect view, until some Hendrix emulators, with massive Afro haircuts, sat three rows in front. This caused a chain reaction, in that girls in the row behind were forced to stand up, and then the girls behind them decided they would have to stand on the arms of their chairs. Andrew and I remained defiantly seated, hoping that a sense of decorum would set in, and somehow reverse the process. However, the fruitlessness of that gesture became apparent as soon as the bands came on, as everyone stood unabashedly. The unshackled screams were contagious and I even felt like screaming myself, at times.

The first band were a gang of Beach Boys doppelgangers, called The Californians. They started a little ropey because they were not used to competing with a wall of hysterical fan-noise. In theory, they were the warm-up band, charged with energizing the audience but they were really the sound-checkers, helping the primitive mixing crew to balance their volume against the crowd mayhem. Their "I Get Around' was decidedly ropey, but the sound -mixer's magic was such that, Barbara Anne was acceptable and the tight harmony of California Girls, was just about perfect.

Cat Stevens was a heartthrob of all teenage girls and when he lurched onto the stage adorned in a red velvet suit, three girls virtually knocked Andrew and I over, to push past us and race, like religious fanatics toward their idol. Luckily, bouncers prevented them from launching, like missiles, onto the stage to try and touch their messiah. As Cat sang "I'm gonna get me a gun," he indulged young women by reaching from the stage, over the bouncer's heads to hold hands with each swooning girl. Next, he gave an excellent rendition of a song that only a dog-owner could appreciate, called, "I love my dog, as much as I love you." He finished with a previously unheard mini-opera called 'Matthew and Son,' about the mundanity of small town factory life. However, the depth of his 'story' was somewhat wasted on the screaming masses. His weird song about Dog-loving was probably a better fit.

As Cat took his bow and backed politely off the stage, he would be forgiven for feeling that he was casting pearls before swine. That the audience was an untameable mass, dominating the show. However, that was just about to change. The least known of the pop acts, young Jimi Hendrix walked on as surreptitiously as the previous act had backed off. Andrew and I looked into each other's eyes, psychically locked in a moment of blissful anticipation. The crowd lulled, as the apparently shy man with a psychedelic shirt and afro-hair clicked his jack plug into his left-handed white Fender

Stratocaster. Feedback screamed out, as if the Californian's sound check had been in vain, and the instinct would normally be to turn the guitar away from the speaker. But Hendrix smiled and leaned into the speaker, and took control of the feedback, playing with the sound with suggestive pelvic movements, as it built he spun around and launched into the introduction to Foxy Lady. The transition from introvert to extrovert was brilliant. He was in control of the music, of the stage, of the audience. Nobody in that audience had seen or heard anything like it. There was a new form of music in our midst, that would change the world forever. The song was wild and every girl in the crowd wanted to be that sexy 'Foxy Lady' that Jimi was singing about. His bass-player and drummer just followed along as Jimi worked the crowd like a sheepdog works sheep. He ended with feedback, which he quickly tamed, like putting the genie that he had released back into the bottle. Andrew and I were ecstatic, and I had the even greater knowledge that I had made it possible. There could only be one person in that room enjoying this rhapsody more than me and my brother, and that was Jimi, himself. Without allowing enough pause to soak up adulation, Hendrix switched guitars to an old Vox panther, and announced, "Let me stand next to your fire," and sure enough, half way through the song, he threw his guitar down and pulled out a can of lighter fuel. He kneeled at the guitar and lit it, coaxing and taunting the flames, as the band kept the song going. Suddenly, a bouncer ran onto the stage with a fire extinguisher and put out the flames, while a roadie handed him back his Stratocaster. The unmistakable opening notes of Purple Haze emerged from the smoke and feedback, and when he stopped for the immortal line "Scuse me while I kiss the sky!" we all chanted it in unison. Half way through the solo, he suddenly diverted into a wailing version of 'Strangers in the Night,' proving that he could make anything sound fantastic. I sensed that everyone was only getting 3 songs, and I felt a dread as he wound up the last notes of Purple haze. But then the crowd demanded an encore, and he played "Hey Joe" alternating between playing the guitar solo behind his head to doing it with his teeth. I was left breathless and changed forever.

I almost felt sorry for Englebert Humperdink, as he bounced onto the stage with his fat lips and white ruffled shirt. Having to follow Jimi, the world's most unique and coolest performer, would have been a challenge for anyone. He opted for an upbeat number, where he shook maracas as he sang "Dance to my ten guitars," If he was trying to harness Jimi's energy, he had no chance, and his ironic choice of songs just seemed pathetic. However, he followed up with his number one ballad, "Please, Release Me" and his own entourage of fans, began to swoon, and then scream. The tour group certainly seemed to have something for everybody. I even felt myself swaying in three/four time as he finished up with The Last Waltz.

While the performers alternated, their appearance order each day, the Walker Brothers remained top of the bill. They were the biggest selling group of the year but they seemed to be just 'going through the motions,' as they droned out one hit after another. I wondered if they secretly wished that they could have gotten on the stage before the phenomenon, The Jimi Hendrix Experience, stole their thunder. The name experience seemed somewhat pretentious before I saw him perform but by the end it was the only logical way to describe my hero and his band. I would not have traded even a Beatles concert, with the memory of the Jimi Hendrix Experience!

"My life is complete!" said Andrew on the bus home.

"Mine too!" was all I could think to add. I had a new purpose in life.

Chapter 21: Boothroyd

As much as my new experiences were heralding my transition to adulthood, there was a teacher who, through a series of misunderstandings, felt it his prime obligation to keep me subjugated with self-loathing. His name was Boothroyd!

Boothroyd was an old-fashioned eccentric. He was one of the few teachers who still wore black robes and a mortar board to school. Underneath this he wore a three-piece Harris tweed suit, with a hand-watch on a chain, which tucked neatly into his waistcoat pocket.

While some teachers needed to shout, or throw books and board erasures, to gain your attention, Mr. Boothroyd was different. He was willing to stand and wait until the class worked out that they were supposed to be silent. Then he would launch into a heavily sarcastic, cleverly humiliating statement that would strip you of self-esteem for weeks.

On one occasion, Boothroyd decided that my exercise book was looking 'somewhat scraggy.' I could never maintain pristine exercise books, and my English notebook was no different. So, when the previous marked assignments were given back out, Boothroyd had written, "COVER THIS BOOK!" in large flamboyant capital letters. When I showed Darren Trainor it tickled him, and Trainor was a brilliant impressionist, amongst other things. He repeated the phrase, over and over, in the unambiguous voice tone that Boothroyd intended. Trainor's impression tickled me every time, too.

They say that, subconsciously, there are no such things as mistakes. However, what I did next was certainly counter to my intentions. In the same ostentatious style as my teacher, I wrote, "NO!" directly under his emphatic command.

"You're bloody mad!" Trainor gasped.

"Well I'll bloody remember to cover it now, won't I!" I retorted.

"There's method in your madness, Kimosabe," Trainor responded, as if he had suddenly become the Lone Ranger's sidekick, Tonto.

Unfortunately, my defining feature, that the family called awkward streak kicked in. It was just a combination of procrastination and forgetfulness but my mum always saw it as passive aggressiveness.

There was a buzz of excitement, as we entered Boothroyd's English class and noticed the cane and punishment book sitting on his desk. I was excited too because it was always good to witness a teacher's caning technique for the first time. Teachers usually bent you over and gave you 'three-of-the-best' non-sadistic, punitive swishes with the birch. However, they could also go for the hold-your-hand out option. The perversity of that one, was that every time you followed your reflexes and pulled the hand away, an extra stroke would be added.

We had all witnessed the cutting barbs of Boothroyd's ruthless sarcasm but a teacher's reputation was 'on the line' when he employed public flogging to reinforce control. If Boothroyd was feeling aggressive, there was no outward display. He often just handed the books to a pupil to distribute but on this occasion, he was calling students out one at a time to make comment on their essays. He was basically just reading out whatever he had written.

"Brown, come here!" he would say. Brown, who had once been caned by Rocky Timpson for "Contaminating the atmosphere," after farting out loud, was visibly relieved when Boothroyd told him, "Some interesting adjectives"

"Bagnall, you seem to be 'padding out your work' with redundant phrases." Boothroyd said.

"Thank you, sir," Bagnall replied

"Good grief, boy, that's not a compliment." the teacher added. He raised an eyebrow, in anticipation of what the boy would say next. Bagnall made a side-glance at the cane on the table and made no further sound.

As each student received his assignment with varying degrees of humiliation, I began to realize that my scraggy, uncovered book was on the bottom of the pile. I was so relieved when Boothroyd's mood was light and jovial by the time he got to me, and I was practically elated when he started to compliment my work.

"Wells, this is really rather good," he started.

"Thank you, sir" I replied. The assignment was to write an essay, starting with the opening lines, "Tis a fearful creature indeed, Sir Jasper......."

Most pupils had written a story about a scary gorilla, in the vein of King Kong. But I had recently watched an old science fiction film called Forbidden Planet, where the surprise twist had been described as "monsters from the Id." The Id is a part of the brain. Therefore, rather than go down the standard path of a beast escaping his cage and attacking innocent victims, I developed a story about 'mind-creatures' that could jump from one person's mind to another. I really enjoyed writing the assignment and appreciated that my teacher liked it. He even had me read it out to the class, which I did with pride.

"Excellent!" he told me. However, as I began my walk back to my desk, Boothroyd said, "Oh Wells, there's something else I would like you to read." The class hushed as they detected the slight change in his tone.

"Can you read what it says on the front of your exercise book, please?"

"COVER THIS BOOK! sir" I nervously read.

"Is there anything else written on the book?" he asked.

"No sir," I responded, as he took the book back off me to scrutinize it more closely.

"There,' he said, pointing to the crossed out "No."

"No sir" I said.

"You mean 'No' there's nothing written there, or 'No' is written there." he was enjoying entertaining the class at my expense.

There's nothing written there because I crossed it out sir.

"But you did write, 'No!' before you crossed it out?"

"Yes sir," I said.

"Oh, you wrote "Yes?"

"No sir, I wrote, 'No' sir. Sorry sir. I thought it would remind me to cover the book but then I forgot."

"Well it seems you need a better reminder system, Wells" he stated, "touch your toes."

I bent over as much as I could and was relieved that he did not push the toe-touching anomaly that I could never achieve.

His four-step run up enhanced his prowess with the class, as I grimaced with each of the three strokes. I held back the tears as he painstakingly wrote in the punishment book. "Insolence and insubordination." Then he handed me the book and cane and said, "Take these to the office."

The kind school office lady, who had seen me in tears over a burst eardrum earlier in the year, saw me again, with gushing tear ducts.

"What on earth's wrong?" she asked, before noticing the cane and book.

"Mr. Boothroyd asked me to bring this back to the office," I explained. As I was leaving I heard her say, "Bloody barbarian." It was comforting to hear some sympathy because most pupils admired this 'perverse prick,' as Andrew later described him.

Two weeks after the public flogging, Alfie Brown acquired a form list and decided to run a popularity survey for all our teachers. Every pupil was asked to give a score to every teacher.

Despite Downing's previous water torture episode, I gave him a handsome 95%, because I could see that he liked me really, and he had laid off me since the varicose veins debacle of injustice. I think I was the only one to give Twee 100%, because his speech impediment was taken into account by most pupils. With the slightest of smugness, I awarded Boothroyd 13%; I felt that this was far more offensive than a straight zero because it showed that I had considered my judgement. It was fascinating to see how the different personalities scored the teachers. Tattersfield, Mary and the other victims, gave the best scores to the strict teachers. Presumably, they felt safest in their classrooms, or they enjoyed the comeuppances as these bully teachers bullied the bullies. Class clowns, like Whittle and Adams, liked the tolerant teachers, who would use humour to diffuse a situation.

Westwood got many zero's but I remembered his compassion on eardrum day and gave him a respectable 70%. There was some validity to the poll because Hardman, whose laziness was only surpassed by his sadistic streak, scored lowest of all. Hovis, scored lowly, as well. He probably did not know one of our names. Boothroyd won, hands down, much to my disappointment.

Now, it never occurred to me, when Alfie Brown, was interviewing me, that these numbers were ever going to get back to the teachers. However, sycophant that Brown was, he decided to tell Boothroyd that he was the unofficial Teacher of the Year. I expected Boothroyd to have acted contemptuously toward this nonsensical vote. However, even this most self-assured teacher was not impervious to flattery. His face was a picture as Alfie handed him the full list of votes.

"Hmmmmmm, Bagnall, I never knew you cared," he responded, as his eyes rolled down the alphabetical list.

"I love English, sir," Bagnall brown-nosed. It was a clever reply because Boothroyd took it as a personal compliment, whereas Bagnall could claim that his loyalty was to the subject and he was not being a teacher's pet.

"Can't think that you love English, Jones. I thought that you just liked grabbing balls," he told the school goalkeeper. "Yet you 'scored' me highly, if you'll pardon the pun."

You could see Jones's mind working overtime, trying to match the teacher's whimsy but after a painstaking silence all he could come up with, "Don't get a chance to score very often, sir."

"Hmmmm… it seems your physical dexterity surpasses your mental agility," commented the sarcastic teacher, purely for his own entertainment.

Jones thought hard again before saying, "Thank you, sir."

"Pearls before swine," Boothroyd quietly told himself, which was his most common utterance.

Whittle and I were starting to sweat as he got down the list. It was like we were the only ones who saw his truly narcissistic nature. If he was tearing apart the pupils who voted for him, what would he do to the antagonists?

"Whittle," he said, squeezing maximum contempt from the syllable. I was secretly crossing my fingers that Whittle didn't put him in a bad mood.

"That's me," replied Whittle, unable to resist his inner rebel.

"Hmmmmm… it is your name, indeed," he admitted. "Seems you feel that I have no redeeming qualities."

"Well you don't hold a grudge, sir," said Whittle, trying to lighten the teacher's mood, with a clever retort.

Boothroyd stopped and mused for a moment before replying almost inaudibly, "Mmmm………. We'll see about that."

"*Great,*" I thought to myself, "*Whittle has kept him sweet.*"

"Wells. You obviously put some thought into your score. Still feeling a little sore, are we?" he asked, obviously referring to my recent caning.

"No, sir," I replied. There was no satisfactory answer.

"No, Wells?" he replied, in a tone that suggested he had drawn me into a trap. "You do seem to enjoy using that word! Would you like to explain to the class how you came to that lowly, yet precise number thirteen?"

"No, sir!" I told him.

"It was a rhetorical question, Wells. Do you even know what a rhetorical question is Wells?"

"No, sir," I admitted.

"You really do seem to enjoy that word, Wells."

"No sir," I responded, much to my own embarrassment and the amusement of the class. I was sweating profusely.

"Well it means that it's not so much a question as a command. So, let's make it easier for you. Why did I score thirteen?"

"Don't know, sir," I explained.

"Do you have some affinity to the Baker's dozen? he asked.

I knew that he could see my unnatural sweating mechanism working overtime, and that he would happily keep me on edge until I was swimming in my own puddle of perspiration. So, I said, "Unlucky for some, sir."

"What are you babbling about now, boy." asked the teacher.

"Well I played a lot of bingo last summer, sir and the bingo caller used to shout, Unlucky for some, thirteen."

The class laughed in unison, especially Whittle, which encouraged my latent awkward streak to throw in a few more quotes from Prestatyn. "Two fat ladies, eighty-eight; knock on the door, number four; a duck and a flea, twenty-three: sunset strip, seventy-seven; all the ones, legs eleven." I added the obligatory wolf whistle accompaniment, assuming I had already surpassed the point of earning another public flogging. I was halfway through my sexy whistle when the teacher cracked.

"Enough!" screamed the ever-calm Boothroyd. There was a communal gasp from the class, as they all turned their attention from me to the teacher. Then, he regained composure and in a controlled voice, "Sit down, idiot!" he said in supercilious tones.

A few years earlier, my brother had taught me something, which had always stuck in my mind.

His theory was that, when two people are in conflict, contrary to popular belief, it was the one that lost his temper who also lost the fight. So, when my mum used to end up yelling at my dad, out of frustration, he was the winner. By the logic of my brother, who I had never known to be wrong, I had just become the unlikely victor in a battle of wits against my arch-nemesis, Boothroyd. However, when I retold the event Andrew explained that Boothroyd was canny enough to lose the battle, only to later win the war. He told me that I should take great care not to inflame the teacher further. Unfortunately, even though I had gained more control over my awkward streak, in recent years, it had no regard for great care, whenever it did kick in.

22. Biddulph Moor

Whilst my dad was delighted to climb the social ladder without so much as a downward glance, mum saw it as her parental duty to keep us grounded. She had always felt obligated to counterbalance Nana Lena's outlandish snobbery. My grandmother could not even say 'Sutton Green,' without curling her lip. In contrast, there was positive anal clenching, whenever she said 'Penkville.'

Mum and dad had opposing views of their social ascent. Dad insisted that our climb out of poverty, was achievable by anyone 'with a bit of nouse.'

"It's survival-of-the-fittest, Beryl," he pointed out.

"That's Darwin's Theory," Andrew interjected.

"Very good, son," said dad, "I'm keeping the species strong!" Dad had recently watched a documentary series, by Desmond Morris, called 'The Naked Ape.' The author claimed that competition between humans was no different to that in monkeys.

"Well, if your mother gave all the other 'chimps' in Sutton Green a thousand quid and a car, I'm sure they'd all be buying semi's in Penkville!"

mum added. She could never resist the chance to temper his ego. My mother felt that it was her calling to 'give back' to those less fortunate; she also wanted us to remember our roots.

"Why don't you invite Tony and Barry over?" Mum insisted, making sure to avoid extending the invitation to Jimmy Drinkwater. I think that she viewed Jimmy's family as being outside the bounds of redemption.

We had not seen Tony in four months, since escaping Sutton Green. Andrew missed him because he was like a complimentary foil; Tony was as practical as Andrew was academic. For example, Andrew knew all about the laws of physical science and nature but Tony had an instinct for making things. Where Andrew was working out the order of levers needed to lift an object, Tony would have already found a big wooden post and have rolled a stone fulcrum into position. Whilst Andrew knew the life cycles of barn owls, Tony could track down their 'coughed up' pellets and tell you whether they had eaten voles, shrews or rats, just by looking at the undigested bones. They were not particularly competitive, because they had different skills, but they were strongest when working together.

I still saw Barry at school regularly but there had always been a different dynamic between our school and home friendships. Barry was in the year above me and, whilst he was known to be a class clown in his own school world, I had to show deference to his extra year of high school experience. I missed 'home Barry' because we had a magical bond from our early childhood days, when we used to become almost hypnotically engrossed in fantasy games with a toy Teddy and Panda. Sometimes we'd catch each other's eye, in school assembly, and give knowing looks. Barry had been the mood-raiser of our gang when we were younger and we missed him.

So, when I extended my mum's invitation, for Barry and Tony, to spend a weekend at our new house, I was delighted that he came back next day, with an even better idea. Tony's uncle had a small dairy farm on Biddulph Moor and we were all going to camp there, at the weekend. All we needed was our sleeping bags. Tony had the tent, camping stove, food and survival equipment.

We synchronised a plan, where we would catch the Chell bus in Stoke and they would alight outside the Sutton Arms, near Smallthorne. As we awaited the bus, I could see Andrew's excitement build, savouring the thought of our reunion with our 'working class' friends. He bought a pack of 20 Embassy filtered cigarettes and we were so early that we had time to smoke two each. It was a relief when our bus pulled up opposite the Sutton Arms and our two friends hoisted their rucksacks up the stairs of the red double-decker. The clanging of billycans seemed to annoy the PMT bus conductor, as each tin vessel crashed against the narrow stairwell.

"Two halves to Chell," said Tony. He was only fourteen, which still qualified him for half-fare, but Tony's immensity made him look more like an eighteen-year-old.

"How old are you?" the conductor asked Tony.

"Fourteen," Tony replied, in total honesty. While we all dreamed of looking older, Tony was sensitive about his precocious growth; he seemed to be three inches higher than when I last saw him. However, nobody in the gang ever alluded to his size.

"When were you born?" the conductor tried to catch him out.

"When the muscles of my mother's birth canal contracted," Tony joked. He had obviously paid attention in his school's new progressive 'sex education class.'

We all chuckled, which antagonized the conductor further. Tony had obviously missed our audience, and was showing off a little.

"Don't come all smartarse, with me," the conductor scolded, "When were you born?"

"Five thirty in the morning, "Tony responded waggishly.

Barry gave out a rip-roaring snort, reminding me of past hilarities and triggering my giggle response.

Tony's reply took the conductor aback and inflamed him further. He rang the bell, and yelled to the driver. "Looks like we're dropping off at the next stop, George!"

Then he turned to Tony and said, "I'll ask you one last time. In which year were you born, you cheeky little sod?"

"Oh, 1953," Tony explained, like he had only just understood the question.

After the conductor went back downstairs, Barry said, "Crash the ash, somebody."

Andrew was proud to hand out four Embassy, which we each gripped between our lips, waiting for him to strike a match. However, the conductor must have sensed that we were going to try to smoke and he charged upstairs, endeavouring to catch us 'in the act.' We all managed to palm our cigarettes in the nick of time, and smiled superciliously.

"You boys know that you have to be sixteen to smoke, don't you?" he asked.

"Well my dad's not sixteen, he's thirty-seven, and he smokes, "Barry laughed.

"Better tell him to stop then!" I joined in.

Our sardonic mood must have been insufferable to the conductor and we saw him look up at the button, contemplating ejecting us. We decided not to risk smoking until we had disembarked. As soon as we reached our destination, we quickly lit our fags and, holding them between two fingers, we waved a rude 'Goodbye' to our uniformed nemesis.

The hike up to Biddulph Moor was an ever-steepening incline and it was a relief to arrive at Tony's uncle's field.

"I'll erect the tent!" Barry declared, enjoying his double-entendre, as he spilled the segments of tentpoles onto the ground.

"Make sure you find a flat spot!" insisted Tony. The problem was that any area that was horizontal enough to accommodate a tent was jam-packed with fresh cow pats.

"I think cow's only crap on the flat!" I snickered

"Have you ever tried shitting uphill?" Tony said, matter-of-factly. This really tickled us all for some reason and we were literally falling over in hysterics.

"I'm not sleeping on a cow's latrine," added Andrew, probably trying to impress us with his vocabulary.

"What's a latrine?" I asked, still euphoric.

Eager to demonstrate that he was familiar with the word, Tony asserted, "A shit-hole!"

"Oh, like Sutton Green? "I instinctively retorted, as quick as a flash.

Instant silence told me that I had just made a huge blunder. When we lived in Sutton Green, it was hilarious to refer to it as a 'dump' or 'shit-hole.' But it was now painfully obvious that Andrew and I had lost the right to besmirch our old stomping ground. I looked over at Andrew but his eyes were firmly fixed on the ground. It was a 'can

233

of worms' that I had opened and Tony and Barry's latent resentments instantly surfaced. There were unresolved feelings of abandonment, as well as inverse snobbery issues. I felt like I had just destroyed the entire weekend, with my futile attempt at humour. Glances between Tony and Barry told me that they had had prior conversations about us "thinking we were better." My comment had consolidated that thought.

Tony was not going to break the silence, Andrew was mentally trying to distance himself from me and I looked over at Barry as my only hope.

"I'd rather live in shit than have it come out of my mouth!" Barry reasoned. His tone was perfect.

Tony's serious face cracked and we all laughed with relief. The 'snobs' had been served their comeuppance and order was restored. Barry pulled out a transistor radio, which poignantly broadcast. "Make the World Go Away" by Eddie Arnold. I understood the song in a whole new way as I had just finished wishing that the ground would open and swallow me and the cow's latrine. We all laughed.

Leaving Andrew and Barry to pitch the tent, Tony took me down the hill to meet his uncle farmer and fill the water-carrier. His uncle had an expressionless face, which was somewhat off-putting because all the eye-contact and smiles could not break through the everyday thoughts of the dairy farmer.

"You young 'uns are in the meadow," he told us. His tone made it impossible to tell whether it was a question or a statement. "Cows' favourite."

Tony and I just nodded politely, as if we understood what he was talking about. We filled our water carrier from an outside tap, and were just about to leave when two girls appeared around the corner. Apparently, they were Tony's cousins. They kept whispering to each other, then giggling, which took me straight back to the mockeries of the primary school girls. I felt a blush surge to my face.

"Aren't you going to introduce us, Tony?" said the older girl.

"Mart, these are my cousins Petra and Joanne," said Tony, oblivious to the girls' flirtations. The younger one seemed to be about my age.

"Hello Martin, nice to meet you," they said in unison, and then they both mock-curtseyed, as though they had rehearsed.

I smiled, blushed and nodded awkwardly. Perhaps the country air had thrown me out of my comfort zone because all the skills that I had acquired at the Top Rank seemed to have abandoned me.

"You're very brave, camping in the meadow," said Petra. This seemed a particularly flattering compliment, coming from a fearless farm girl. Joanne snorted out a stifled laugh, like there was a hidden meaning to her sister's comment. Tony seemed a bit confused by their reaction. He had known his cousins all his life but he had never seen them in flirtatious mode before.

The climb back up the hill, with a full gallon water bottle, was gruelling. As the hill got progressively steeper the bottle seemed to get heavier and heavier. I distracted myself by focusing on the exchange between Petra and myself. She truly seemed to admire my bravery and the physical demands on my mind and body consolidated my feelings. By the time, I got to base camp, where Andrew and Barry had been busily erecting the tent, I was stricken with the pangs of love.

"There's girls at the farm!" I blurted out.

"No there's not! They're just cousins!" Tony asserted. He was suddenly being protective; he seemed genuinely to have seen his dad's brother's daughters as asexual beings, up to this moment.

"What are they like?" asked Barry, dropping the mallet that he had been using to drive in tent pegs.

"Mine's nice! Her name's Petra," I replied without thought. Amazingly, nobody challenged my claim.

Once the tent was secured, all that was left was to pin down the ground sheet. Andrew and Barry had allegedly removed eight cow pats from the area that they had selected but the smell of poo lingered in the soil, and the groundsheet did little to limit it. We rolled out our sleeping bags hoping they would quell the rising odours. Tony had a theory that the smell would subside as soon as we got the stove going because the stink of cow dung came from the same gasses as trumps; Tony had allegedly lit farts on a previous camping expedition. So, Tony boiled a billycan of water, on the Calor gas stove and mixed in some instant mash potato powder.

Once we were in the tent we snuggled into our sleeping bags. They had pitched the tent slightly on a slope, in such a way that our legs were a foot lower than our shoulders. There was a definite danger of sliding out of the tent but, if it had been pitched sideways on the slope, everyone would have rolled onto the person at the lowest point, who would undoubtedly have been me.

Once settled, it was time to share stories. We always had an unspoken law, of 'What happens in the tent, stays in the tent.' The first time that we ever camped out was when I was nine years old, in Barry's back yard, and I had declared my undying love for a girl in my class named Sally Doyle. The others shared their secret fantasies back then, and we all kept each other's secrets. Andrew and Tony had both had a crush on Jane Lockett, though ironically, I was the only one that had been kissed by her, at a German Measles party. Barry fancied Tina Carrolla, whose mother had a reputation of being a man-eater and Tina's precocious breast growth unfairly enhanced the theory of 'like mother like daughter!'

"Uhgghh!" we groaned in disgust. But again, Barry's repugnant desire was treated as sacrosanct outside the canvas confessional. The unspoken rules still applied three years later.

I started by embellishing my encounter with the new girl of my dreams, Petra. Barry and Andrew were decidedly jealous and bitter that I had been off flirting with 'sex kittens,' as the ever-evolving yarn had grown. Of course, we were half-convinced that their nymphomania might take such a grip, that the girls would be forced to visit us in the night.

It seemed prudent to reiterate my undying love for Petra to consolidate the group's acceptance.

Tony made the mistake of saying, "I can't see why you like Petra. Joanne's the attractive one!"

This was a big mistake, even within the of the safe environs of the tent.

"Ugggghhhhh!" said Barry and Andrew in unison.

"You can't fancy your cousin!" I added.

Tony blushed and exclaimed, "I never said that I fancied her. I just said she was attractive!"

"Well, technically it's not illegal to marry your cousin, in this country," Andrew explained.

"I don't like my cousin! Tony reasserted.

This triggered Andrew to launch into a mini-lecture on altruism. He explained that it was like a moral code, built into our DNA, which prevents us fancying our direct relatives. Most parts of the world made it illegal to have an interest in anybody genetically closer than a second cousin but England's dedication to keeping royals royal had loosened those rules, perpetuating genetic abominations such as haemophilia and even madness. Andrew had a theory that Jack-the- Ripper had been a secret royal mutant and that the reason that he was never caught was because of the protection of the Crown. He explained how 'outbreeding' kept the race strong and vigorous. Apparently, this was backed by evidence of twenty-three generations of inbred guinea pigs.

"The German's nearly took over the world by inbreeding," Tony threw in.

Still nervous about the perceived class war, Andrew trod lightly but he said, "Tony, Hitler was a bit of a twat!"

"Ha ha," we all chuckled at his understatement.

I threw in a joke, which seemed almost relevant, "What's the height of frustration?"

"Don't know, what is the height of frustration?" they all obliged.

"A tortoise trying to mount a German helmet," I said.

They all groaned but I could tell they liked it.

"I think Petra likes me," I insisted, still a tad love-struck.

Now Tony's protective altruism kicked in and he suddenly declared, "Nobody touches my cousins, okay?!"

We all capitulated and the subject was dropped.

Barry was next to entertain us. He pulled out a pack of cards and made up a new game that he called, 'Sleeping Bag Jack Naked.' It was like the regular game of Strip Jack Naked only, every time a player lost a hand, they had remove an item of clothing, whilst remaining in the sleeping bag.

Ironically, the cards seemed to be stacked against Barry, himself. Andrew laid down a Jack, and Barry's two of diamonds necessitated that he wriggled around his sleeping bag until he finally produced a smelly sock. It was hilarious, until he lobbed it in the air and it landed on my nose.

"Ahhhhh," I screamed, "Get it off, get it off!" My repugnance was only surpassed by their jocularity. Ten minutes later, I was still on high alert, when his underpants sailed past my face.

The pack of cards seemed to know when Barry was fully stripped, and they began to turn their attentions on the rest of us. Soon enough, we were all Houdiniing out of our clothes in our narrow straight-jacket-like sleeping bags. I was getting nervous because I really didn't want the game to progress to naked buckers (dares). I knew that Barry wouldn't care but I was really shy about undressing. I hated communal showers after boys PE classes for that very same reason.

Andrew was shy too, and he decided it was time to clarify the rules. "Once you're naked you lose, and drop out of the game. The winner is the last to be wearing underpants."

We all agreed, just in time, as Andrew's pants took off on the established flight path past my face. Tony was declared the champion, but he wriggled his pants off, anyway, and rubbed them in my face!

"Bugger off!" I yelled.

It was Tony's turn to provide the entertainment, when we were distracted by breathing outside the tent. Then we could hear two discrete breaths and what appeared to be faint whispering.

"It's the girl's! They're going to try and scare us!" said Barry excitedly. He didn't seem to feel the same vulnerability, in his nakedness, as the rest of us. He blew out the candle, which would have made sense if we were planning to regain an advantage, and scare them back. Unfortunately, the pitch black made finding our clothes impossible. It also added an eerie dimension to the 'game.' We could hear them moving around heavily outside, almost as though they wanted us to hear. It sounded like they were trying to pull out the tent pegs and implode the tent. Again, it would have been a great laugh, if we hadn't been trapped, naked, in our sleeping bags.

"I've found the torch," Tony declared. It certainly seemed a better option than relighting the candle, if the tent was about to collapse. We listened to try and work out what Petra and Joanne were up to. I was so uncomfortable that they would discover us unclothed. It would be embarrassing, as well as our nudity requiring some serious explaining.

Suddenly, it became apparent that the girls were at the entrance, and they seemed to be grappling with the ties, ready to dive in and frighten us. If they had used commando tactics to creep up originally, they were now oblivious to the racket they were making as they prepared their surprise attack.

In a loud whisper, Tony said, "On the count of three, I'm putting the torch on. All scream when I do. One………..Two………..Three."

The torch went on.

"Aaaggghhhhhhh," we all screamed at what we thought was the top of our lungs, as we anticipated seeing the two girls' blushing faces in the doorway.

"AAAGGGGHHHHHHHHHH," we now screamed, at an extra twenty decibels above the top of our lungs, as a huge cow's face thrust into our tent. It was a vile snorting dripping mass of terror. The screaming and flashlight had the intended effect of frightening the intruder, alright. But she did not seem to know the best way to deal with it. She started to shake her head so violently that pints of mucus shot from her nostrils covering all of us. The noises that we heard outside, a few minutes earlier were not tent pegs being uprooted by playful teenage girls. It was the sound of a cow ripping up lush blades of grass and swallowing them. Now, she was regurgitating copious amounts of semi-digested cud and spray painting the lining of the tent, while letting rip with a bellow, which proved that her lungs were far bigger than ours. The stench would surely be at home in the bowels of Hell! Next, the tent pegs were pinging high into the air, as she lifted the tent completely off us. I learned in that moment that the instinct of survival surpasses false modesty. As the tent became a blindfold for the terrified bucking cow, our four naked figures, long devoid of our sleeping bag encumbrances, ran for our lives, through a moonless, pitch black dung-filled field.

Tony was the first to regain his senses, "The tent, the tent!" he cried.

"Sod the tent, let's find our clothes!" cried Andrew.

"Shiiiiiiiiit!" shouted Barry and I, as we both squelched barefoot into fresh cow shit.

The commotion must have been audible from the farmhouse because a light came on. Andrew's logic moved up the priority list. Tony brought his flashlight back to the point where just a groundsheet remained and we sought out our clothes. Barry put my underpants on, so I had to wear his. Admittedly, it was gross, but I could see that the cow poo had squirted up between his toes and those feet must had rubbed off on my pant leg-holes. The dressing was more laborious than the initial undressing, even though there were no cards involved.

Even with copious cow crap in my socks, I felt relieved that I had managed to get clothes on my body. The lights went off again in the farmhouse below. The cow, still blindfold with our tent seemed to have regained some dignity and serenity as she stood silent in her canvas bonnet. I was just wondering how we were supposed to retrieve the tent, when its owner, Tony, showed his true heroism. He simply walked up to the cow, and lifted it off, like he was removing a sweater. He did it with such panache, that the cow accepted it. The tent pegs took some retrieving, Andrew found one forty feet from the base, and several had disappeared for ever. However, we worked as a team to resurrect the tent and clean up the mixture of mucus and cud.

Barry re-tuned the transistor to Radio One, only to reveal Lee Dorsey singing, "Holy Cow, what you doing, now?" We all sang along. The song was still reverberating in my brain the next morning, as the horrors of the night before started to consolidate into a hilarious memory.

Chapter 22: Keep on Running!

As Tom Jones was hogging the airwaves, with his mammoth hit about the Green Green Grass of Home, it only served to remind me of Wardle house team colour. Andrew had calculated that there was only a one in sixteen chance of being placed in the same colour team in primary and high school.

Andrew explained, "Odds are meaningless once fate gets involved." I could not question fate, as it was constantly serenading my life through the radio-waves.

Our verdant-shirted team had come an embarrassing last in every house competition, from chess to cricket, over the year. I seemed to be the only viable athlete in the whole house, I was selected to represent them in several events outside my skill set. My high jumping skills also appeared to qualify me for pole vault and triple jump. News got out about my early days as a 60- yard dasher. It was a 'no brainer' to our team manager, Mr Hardman, that someone good at high jump and sprinting, was obviously the perfect selection for the hurdles. Worst of all, the sickness-that-was-named-Hardman decided that a sprinter would be a brilliant selection for the mile.

The day started well. Misters Whippy and Wrench were allowed to drive onto the property for this one day of the year, which gave a carnival atmosphere to the school. Downing had the starting pistol and broke all the gun etiquette rules by pointing it at Tattersfield and Monaghan alternately, although he was wise enough to face it skyward at the last second before firing off blanks. It occurred to me that the teachers had the same instincts to dislike the school victims as the other students.

The morning was very encouraging. The high jump competition was an early event and my mates, Darren Trainor and Jed Stone, had volunteered to be the sandpit-rakers and bar replacers. Their main motivation was to get out of Hovis Brown's final music class of the year.

I had a unique high jump style, with a bouncing five-step run-up. It was not a traditional straddle because, once I launched myself into a completely horizontal position, and my hips had cleared the bar, I spontaneously let my body go limp. My momentum carried me clear and I rotated onto my back like a sack of potatoes.

246

"Fizzing 'eck, Wells! You're an ergonomic disaster! Westwood exclaimed, "you're breaking every rule in the book," he explained.

Trainor chipped in, "I'd like to see that, sir."

"What are you talking about, boy?" asked Fizzer, not recognizing Trainor's deadpan tone as one of humour.

"The Book of Ergonomic Disasters, sir," said Trainor.

"Idiot!" replied Westwood, then "It's like a glorified straddle that inexplicably evolves into a belated Western Roll," Westwood analysed, quite accurately.

"It's called The Waddle," said Trainor, quick as a flash. This comment brought us all to the point of hysterics. Even Fizzer giggled to himself, which nobody had ever seen before.

Of course, it is the nature of high jump, that even the victor ends with three consecutive failed attempts. So, even though I cleared six inches more than any other competitor, setting a new school record, when I did finally fail Fizzer had his 'told you' moment.

"If you could just stick to one or the other styles you could jump higher." said the PE master.

"Sky's the limit, sir" chipped in Trainor.

"Yes," agreed Fizzer, before analysing the statement," then he added, "No, what are you fizzing talking about, idiot boy. What are you even doing here?"

"When Waddle, I mean Wells, knocks it off I put the bar back on. I suppose you could call me the bartender, sir," Trainor retorted.

"I suppose I could call you Smartarse!" Fizzer retorted, chuckling to himself.

"I do have quite a neat bottom, sir but you're the first teacher to comment on it," replied Smartarse Trainor quietly.

Fizzer obviously did not hear Trainor clearly but he knew something cheeky had been said, so he responded, "Your arse will be smarting in a minute, idiot boy!

"Very good, sir, very droll," he told him. Music class was over and Trainor was hoping he could drag out the chore to miss geography and physics, as well. Darren Trainor had managed to avoid the cane throughout his first year at Hartley High and it would have been a shame to lose that record on the last day.

High jump was the highlight of my day. Of course, Hardman thought I would be a natural pole-vaulter but I had no experience in that and I found that the pole added no advantage. In fact, it was a decided handicap and my vault was worse than my 'waddle.'

Trainor lightened my blushes saying, "That was piddle, Waddle!" He always knew when to tease and when to keep quiet, although I did not appreciate the nickname that he was starting to nurture.

The triple jump was just as under-practiced, and the hop, skip and jump event turned out to be a technique that you should not attempt for the first time in live competition. All I had to go on was watching the competitors before me. They seemed to do a short hop, a moderate skip, and then save their main thrust for the jump phase. I should have realized that there was a reason for this. However, I visualized a gold medal to match my high jump triumph. So, I landed an exceptionally long hop but controlling the landing was far trickier than I had anticipated. My hopping leg began to buckle and it took all my strength to launch off into the skip phase. The skip was weak, but that was not its worst feature. I took off at an angle of about 50 degrees to the norm, so that I had to compensate the jump, with a zigzag action which left me on my back just short of the sand pit.

"They should change its name to Hop, Skip and Jesus-who-moved-the-sandpit?" quipped Trainor.

Hilarious as this comment was, I temporarily lost my sense of humour and threw him a dirty look. He made a gesture like he had just been stabbed by the 'daggers' I had sent but then he gave me a friendly nod, showing that he knew he had 'crossed the line' and it was time to stop his commentary.

On my second attempt I overstepped the line, too. I was about three inches past the take-off board. The third effort involve such short hops and skips that the jump only just got me to the sand. At least, it was a jump that could be measured but it still left me in eighth place.

"Good try, Mart," Darren Trainor reassured me and our camaraderie was restored.

By lunchtime, I was ravenous and I was disappointed that the cooks had chosen boiled liver for their year-end 'piece de resistance.' Liver was the one meat the upper schoolers were happy to divvy up equally. I still found it as abhorrent as when nursery's Mrs Flood forced us to 'at least taste it' eight years earlier. To make matters worse, Monaghan suddenly joined me and Trainor and Barry Pratt.

"Sod off, Monaghan!" we all whispered in unison. He was used to the greeting, so he ignored us and sat down anyway. I was about to make a pain-in-the-neck pun, referring to the now-legendary fork incident, when I felt a pair of hands leaning on my shoulders from behind. I instinctively froze and could see from Barry's response that I was right to resist reacting. The pressure on my shoulders increased.

"Do we have a problem here?" came the ultra-calm tones of Boothroyd. It was obvious that he had just heard what we had told Monaghan.

"No sir," we replied in perfect monotone.

"Seems all the comedians have gathered in one spot," he said. "Now what's the collective noun for a group such as this? A pride? No that's lions - there's no pride here? How about a cackle? No that's laughing Hyenas, but I think I'm getting warmer? How about a conspiracy? No I believe that's Lemurs."

Boothroyd was enjoying combining his two favourite things, the eccentricities of the English language and public ridicule of schoolboys. Barry Pratt had never had him as a teacher, so he did not have a particularly good grasp, but Barry had very little tolerance for superciliousness.

As Boothroyd continued amusing himself as to a suitable collective noun for us, Barry chimed in, "Is it a fuck, sir?"

"What did you say?" Boothroyd replied, rather taken aback.

"A flock, sir, Or, is that sheep, sir?" Pratt replied.

"Oh, I thought you said something else," replied Boothroyd.

"I could have done, sir," Pratt continued, despite me trying to silence him with little kicks under the table. "I could have said birds, I suppose. But that's not entirely accurate. I mean, Seagulls flock, but it's a Parliament of Owls, a Murmuration of Starlings, or an Unkindness of Ravens.

We were all aghast at Pratt's knowledge. Apparently, Barry had once earned a gold star for a school project, for Mrs Heath at Marston Road Primary School based on collective nouns and that was something that nobody ever forgot.

251

It was a brilliant moment which took the wind out of Boothroyd's sails and he decided to abandon the topic.

"What about you Mr Monaghan, are you feeling at home, amongst this 'flock' of comedians?

"I'm fine, sir," he lied.

"Monaghan's carbuncles are not helping my appetite, sir," said Pratt.

Boothroyd was obviously amused but could not respond because they weren't really allowed to condone student bullying, despite have free reign to do it themselves.

"Well I'm sure Mr Monaghan would have preferred that you kept those thoughts to yourself, Mr. Pratt," he said.

"I'm just worried he won't keep those pustules to himself, sir. We've got custard to come, sir," Barry replied.

"Uggghhhhhh!" said everyone, including Boothroyd, involuntarily.

There followed an uncomfortable silence, as it became obvious that the confident teacher was flummoxed as to how to respond. At least, the uncomfortableness of the situation caused him to finally release his grip on my shoulders.

He was about to step back when Monaghan suddenly went into a state of pure rage. He grabbed the oven-hot metal food pan and deliberately launched its entire contents, of steaming hot liver and gravy, high into the air. Time seemed to slow down as we watched gnarly lobes of boiled liver succumbing to Newton's Laws of Motion, as the vile brown blobs began to accelerate back down toward earth. I dived for cover but a hot dollop bounced off the back of my neck, causing me to turn, just in time to see Boothroyd losing his footing on a gravy slick. I tried not to laugh as I witnessed an undercooked clump of liver wedge into his beard.

Everyone at the table gave a communal, "Uggggghhhhhh!" as we were all completely bathed in hot liver juice and sloppy onions. A split-second silence was broken by a wave of cheering from all the other tables. The combination of seeing the school bully humiliate himself and the 'coolest' teacher lying in a decidedly uncool puddle of meat was the perfect end to the year. However, as the cheering built to a crescendo, an almost inhuman scream pierced the wall of noise.

"Aaarrgghhhh! Aaarrgghhh! Aaarrgghhh!" screamed Monaghan, as delayed pain of the oven-hot metal pan suddenly hit his sensory system with full force. He threw the pan, randomly, glancing it off Boothroyd's shoulder, and then ran out of the canteen shouting "Shit! Shit! Shit!" blowing on his burned skin.

"His dog might need to use his own paws for a day or two," joked Trainor.

Twee stepped up to quell the crowd, "Everybody keep calm, there is weally nothing to see here," he announced. Having been privy to some of my Chemistry mishaps over the year, Twee had learned to keep his head when all around were losing theirs'. "Mr. Boothroyd's not hurt, except for his pwide."

There was something momentarily satisfying in seeing my favourite teacher take control of a situation that my least favourite has lost. However, as Boothroyd pulled himself up, our eyes met. In that split-second I knew that he held me responsible for the humiliation that had befallen him. Whatever his initial plan, when he had rested his hands upon my shoulder, the intimidation that was intended for me had turned back on himself. While Barry's part in the fiasco probably went unpunished, Monaghan would probably be tracked down and caned. I had an ominous feeling that my life would be tormented by my arch-nemesis when school started up after the six-week holiday.

After lunch, the whole school took to the embankment, and half of them seemed to have portable transistor radios. The embankment oversaw the finish line of the track. While only Darren Trainor had witnessed my morning success in the high jump there were nine hundred excited boys ready to cheer for their house and mock opposing teams. Wardle house was particularly easy to ridicule.

I learned that the hurdles also, was not an event that you should attempt for the first time in front of an audience of mocking peers. I was glad to bow out in fifth place of the first heat, whilst their focus was more attuned to Radio One.

The hundred-yard sprint also taught me something about myself. From the gun, I quickly made up for my slow start and by the halfway mark I was looking to be cruising to victory, re-enacting my sprinting triumphs from Junior School days. However, I discovered that my 'sprint muscle' fibres all simultaneously fatigued, at the sixty-yards point and the last part of the race seemed to take place in slow motion.

Even with my personal disappointments of the day, the carnival atmosphere kept spirits high; between events, we were having a whale of a time on the embankment. Garry Walters, the school minstrel, had bought his guitar and he was singing Jimi Hendrix's "Hey Joe," over and over. I felt the same feeling that I had had when the nurses had played my guitar at my parent's house-warming party. I determined that I would learn to play guitar during the rapidly approaching summer holidays. Smokers were also taking the opportunity to secretly indulge; despite the high profile mingling of some of the teachers, a strong burning tobacco smell permeated the whole grassy bank.

There were numerous gorse bushes all over the hillock, which kept the likes of Tattersfield very guarded. The thorns of a gorse were so sharp that they could inflict serious damage if a 'playful mob' took it upon themselves to lob you into a bush.

I had learned from Downing's biology class that gorse had a unique way of dispersing their seeds. They grew in a pod, and as the casing became dry, it would suddenly rip open and fire black seeds many feet away from the parent plant. The afternoon sun was a perfect temperature for activating this mechanism, resulting in a permanent machine-gun sound. If we had been in Twee's science lab, he would have been insisting that we wore goggles because the randomly dispersing seeds seemed to head straight for unprotected eyes. It felt like a crowd of bullies had been issued pea-shooters, and several fights broke out because of mistaken assumptions. If the pole vault, triple jump, and sprint events had been 'reality checks' for my ego, my self-esteem had one last hurdle to encounter: the mile!

Despite my lack of 'stamina fibres,' Hardman had selected me and Mary to represent Wardle. Two runners from each house meant that, even securing seventh and eighth place would gain three points between us. Tattersfield had been selected as the second Mitchell representative, so I was likely to come no worse that sixth.

As Downing fired the starting pistol, Woolbridge, his sidekick, fastidiously clicked his stopwatch. Tatty went for temporary glory, by setting off at an unsustainable canter, while us wiser ones plodded at a more realistic pace. However, it served the purpose of focusing the whole crowd's attention. They openly cheered. After three hundred yards, the gravitational pull of the pack started to exert its pull on Tattersfield like reeling in a fish and he was already in last place by the time we passed the finish line for the first time.

"One minute, forty-three," announced Woolbridge the lap counter.

Apparently, this was too slow for the serious contenders and Barber, the leader, moved up a gear, taking the top five runners away in a seemingly effortless burst. By the end of the second lap they were two hundred yards ahead. I hit 'the wall,' with still half the race to go but Mary and Tatty were a good fifty yards back from me and I could guarantee three points for Wardle by 'simply' completing the race.

The overall contest between Mitchell, the blues, and the red-shirted Harrison team was tighter than previous years. Hughes of the blues, was clinging to the shoulder of the favourite Barber, the red. This created a buzz of excitement.

Then, Fizzer Westwood picked up the megaphone and raised it to his lips and announced, "The Whole House Championship rests on this race. Mitchell have 406 points, Harrison have 403." Suddenly, the pack of five accelerated. I continued to plod, with my legs feeling heavier with each stride. Fizzer's announcement had the opposite effect on Mary and Tatty. They accepted their role as losers, and they began walking and chatting a good 60 yards behind me.

257

As fatigue set in, I deliberately tried to distract my mind away from the leg pain. A thought flashed through my head, that the year's most prominent victims, Mary and Tatty, had suddenly become united in the face of adversity. They were probably delighted that it was their last day of school and their tormentors would be disappearing from their lives for the next six weeks. However, unlike bullies, I'd never witnessed victims bonding. They usually had no more empathy for their fellow sufferers than the persecutors. So, as the lactic acid build up in my muscles forced me to trudge around lap three at snail pace, I was formulating a theory about bullies and victims. Perhaps the pain made my philosophy feel more profound but I felt like I had discovered the secret of humanity. Neither bullies, nor victims, had any empathy. I thought back to the conversations with my brilliant elder brother, about empathy, as I forced my body onwards. Then, a particularly apt phrase that he had used sprang to mind with ironic clarity. Andrew had once explained empathy to me, as being the ability to imagine how somebody else feels.

He had quoted a famous proverb "You can only understand another person when you have walked a mile in their shoes!" That was basically what Tatty and Mary were doing- walking a mile, sharing a common sufferance.

My mind was jerked quickly back into reality, as the crowd began to cheer madly. We were on the home straight and the three leaders were milking every last muscle fibre, lapping me as they jostled for their finish line.

Hughes of the blues was sitting right on Barber's shoulder, threatening a last second upset. Woolly Bully leaned over the side-line, intent on clocking the winner to the nearest millisecond, and nine hundred Hartliensians suddenly became very patriotic to their houses.

"Hughes, Hughes, Hughes," yelled all the blues.

"Barber, Barber!" the reds reciprocated.

No one cheered for the Greens but it felt momentarily good to be part of the affair.

At the line, Hughes's dip clinched victory and eight points for Mitchell, seven for Harrison. However, with the other red clinching fourth place and Mitchell's Tattersfield in joint last place with over a lap to go, it looked like Harrison would win by a clear point. Perhaps, more points if Tatty and Mary's conversation included the futility of bothering to finish.

The bell rang annoyingly loudly as I closed the finish line for the penultimate time, snapping me out of my philosophical daydream. As the cheering subsided, I noticed the combined effect of a couple of hundred transistor radio's blasting out Spencer Davis classic song. "Keep on Running!" Radio One seemed obliged to team up with fate to orchestrate the last day of the school year. I wanted to explain to Stevie Winwood, the band's singer, that the speed I was attaining would not qualify for the description of 'running.' My lungs gasped, punishing me for a year of smoking. Worse still, I could feel my heart pounding in my chest and the agony in my legs was unbelievable.

The ache of muscle fatigue launched my mind back to the bike trip to Manifold Valley the previous summer. It seemed that I had been so young back then. I'd gone through puberty since and cringed at the very thought that I had blubbered like a baby. I thought about how I had used my transition to high school to change my image in terms of girls. I no longer blushed like I used to in Primary School. After a flirting session with Linda Harley, when I took my 'sister' to the park, I had gone on to enjoy regular snogging sessions at the Top Rank. I recalled how I had developed a huge crush on a farm girl that I had only met for about a minute, I started to think about the mysteriousness of love. These distracting thoughts carried me another hundred yards but the leg pains were becoming excruciating and it was hard to imagine how I was going to cover the last three hundred.

My brain was also starting to lack oxygen at this point and I had learned from Downing that this organ does not function well, anaerobically! Andrew had once told me that people's lives flash before their eyes, as they are dying. I had a definite empathy as a myriad of memories cascaded through my brain, I continued to ponder my life over the last year.

I glimpsed Wrench's Ice Cream van from the corner of my eye, and I began to muse that adults were flawed. The childishness of Beano and Wrench had been an eye-opener for me. It was also the year that Andrew had shown a darker side. Drunken condom-inflating exploits on the infamous Austria trip and his further alcohol-induced behaviour at my parents' party had left him both tainted and admired in my eyes. I wondered if this meant that he would be an alcoholic one day.

I thought about the *loco parentis* role of teachers, which meant that they had the rights of any 'reasonable parent.' Surely, the NSPCC would have taken Hardman's children off him, if he tortured and maimed them like he had Fatty Witherspoon. I also rationalized that Boothroyd's cynical barbs were 'emotional cruelty' but child protection agency would probably let him keep his children. Boothroyd had ruined the art of sarcasm for me; I was beginning to understand why people called it the 'lowest form of wit.'

Every sweat gland opened, as my body's thermostat identified a new problem: overheating. I thought about how the kind-hearted teachers, like Twee, were preyed upon and exploited by the predatory students. It led back to my thoughts about bullies and victims. How I had been kinder-than-most to the pair of class victim's, who were chumming up some way behind me. I had ended up having to throw Tattersfield over a wall to rectify my mistake and Mary had burst my eardrum in

261

payment for my efforts. Any thoughts of feeling sorry for them evaporated, as I recalled those happenings. I was halfway around the last lap and I told myself that the next hundred yards might be the hardest. I would really need to take my mind away from my failing body systems, if I was to complete the task.

I considered how the world around me was changing, as boy's hair grew longer, especially sideburns, and about the exciting musical revolution. I reflected on the first time I had heard Jimi Hendrix playing Purple Haze. I had no idea what the song was about but I could identify with fuzzy vision as the oxygen deprivation to my brain kicked in. I felt like I was about to pass out. But then a hundred transistor radios came back into earshot as Spencer Davis continued to tell me to "Keep on Running!" I could feel my heart pounding in my neck and I toyed with the idea of walking the last stretch. I glanced behind, to check the progress of the last placed duo; It would be fitting if they had formed a pact to cross the line together, celebrating their freshly acquired empathy.

To my horror, the walk had helped them recover, and they were now jogging, closing the gap to twenty yards. The crowd rose to their feet and cheered, as these two most unlikely heroes strived to pip me to the post. Each had humiliated me once during the year but this would be a disaster.

Then Fizzers voice on the megaphone blasted out, "If Tattersfield can clinch sixth place, then Mitchell will beat Harrison by a point."

Suddenly, a year of image building was about to be destroyed as the two victims poised to take my scalp! They had the momentum and I started to feel their gravitational pull on my back. I could hear their asthmatic wheezing becoming louder, as we hit the final straight. With just sixty yards to go, the two rivals drew level with my shoulder. Their trotting was completely synchronized and it seemed to give them a strength that they were enjoying for the first time in their lives. Even though I could hardly see, as my eyes were rolling up in my head, the crowd reaction told me that I was in a position of total humiliation. A couple of years earlier I had been unbeatable over 60 yards but that was when I had not already covered 1,700 yards. With 35 yards to go, it looked like the two rivals really had formed an unspoken agreement to cross the line together, in equal sixth place.

So many thoughts swamped my mind, I would have been cheering for the underdogs myself, if it was anyone other than me that they had just left in their dust. I admired their alliance. If all the victims could realize the power of unity, then bullies would never dare to attack them. However, Mary's lack of integrity shone through, with twenty yards to go. The glory of the finish line ahead became irresistible and he broke synch with

Tattersfield, unexpectedly quickening his step. I was a beaten man, wondering how I could ever face the world, when a miracle occurred: Tattersfield took Mary's last-minute betrayal hard, and five yards from the line he launched himself, full length, latching both hands onto Mary's ankles. Luckily, I was far enough behind to side-step the ensuing brawl and I collapsed over the line in sixth place. Mary jumped up to claim seventh place and Tattersfield, who would probably have been disqualified if it had mattered, was reduced to eight place. A mass of red-shirted Harrison team-members raced to help me and Mary to our feet. Suddenly, our green-shirts were enjoying the adulation of the red team. My high jump triumph may have gone almost unnoticed but my sixth place in the mile would be remembered and talked about for years to come.

On the first Monday morning of the six-weeks holiday, I lay in bed, in our Penkville house, thinking about how everything had changed in my life - home, school, friends. Everyone in the family was different. Mum had become a nurse and learned to drive. Andrew had tarnished his perfect image, by becoming more rebellious, with acts such as smoking and drinking. Except for being a proud house owner, my dad had stayed consistent. I felt like I had grown in every aspect of my life. I was taller and had a little hair under my arms. I felt more confident, or at least less shy, around girls. I was starting to form opinions of my own and develop philosophies, like my elder brother. I had gained more control over my awkward streak, except for the procrastination - I had been putting off working on that. Music had become a massive part of my life.

I heard mum, get up and put on the kettle and the radio.

Tony Blackburn chuntered, "Well here's a blast-from-the-distant-past! Who remembers this fellow? Its Keith West singing 'Excerpt from a Teenage Opera."

"Count the days, into years........." sang one-hit-wonder, Keith West. Doodle and I snuggled under my covers, and I realized that nothing had really changed at all.

The End

Discography.

Except from a Teenage Opera (Keith West)
https://www.youtube.com/watch?v=wAyGMLx_CSo
Monday Monday (Mamas and the Papas)
https://www.youtube.com/watch?v=CKuMMXUROrE
Out of Time (Chris Farlow)
https://www.youtube.com/watch?v=LMli47EQVWE
Keep on Running (Spencer Davis Group)
https://www.youtube.com/watch?v=g7iypCOIGCk
Dedicated Follower of Fashion (The Kinks)
https://www.youtube.com/watch?v=QA5gJ0hZpCc
Return to Sender (Elvis Presley)
https://www.youtube.com/watch?v=LZmUfUBqE-s
Sloop John B (The Beach Boys)
https://www.youtube.com/watch?v=HW5yLvoJMD4
Summer Holiday (Cliff Richard)
https://www.youtube.com/watch?v=rbNP5yqg7hc
Flowers in the Rain (The Move)
ttps://www.youtube.com/watch?v=_laosNxqzNg
Fire Brigade (The Move)
https://www.youtube.com/watch?v=UVys3YPRLWk
Yellow Submarine (The Beatles)
https://www.youtube.com/watch?v=FZLIcQf47TQ
My Ship is Coming In (The Walker Brothers)
https://www.youtube.com/watch?v=df-486gNEgM
World Cup Willie (Lonnie Donegan)
https://www.youtube.com/watch?v=TA3btKkbZpU
I'm a Boy (The Who)
https://www.youtube.com/watch?v=GgOyqdN2SaE
Day Tripper (The Beatles)
https://www.youtube.com/watch?v=jDm2soD0UFE

266

Black is Black (Los Bravos)
https://www.youtube.com/watch?v=BvFwdD7aW1M
Standing in the Shadows (Rolling Stones)
https://www.youtube.com/watch?v=BvFwdD7aW1M
Working in a Coalmine (Lee Dorsey)
https://www.youtube.com/watch?v=3Dy2tuF915E
Sound Of Silence (The Bachelors)
https://www.youtube.com/watch?v=1RYh4hAmFZ4
God Only Knows (The Beach Boys)
https://www.youtube.com/watch?v=uEomFTVGxo4
Sunny Afternoon (The Kinks)
https://www.youtube.com/watch?v=8WRoLfJ1nRA
Pretty Flamingo (Manfred Man)
https://www.youtube.com/watch?v=28_gnIoXAnA
All or Nothing (The Small Faces)
https://www.youtube.com/watch?v=dfhSdB2ZsN8
The Sun Ain't Gonna Shine (Walker Brothers)
https://www.youtube.com/watch?v=Q11ium_-Lv8
Strangers in the Night (Frank Sinatra)
https://www.youtube.com/watch?v=hlSbSKNk9f0
Boots were Made for Walking (Nancy Sinatra)
https://www.youtube.com/watch?v=GX8JaQ65D20
March of the Mods (Joe Loss Orchestra)
https://www.youtube.com/watch?v=CT6HMbprr9E
Hunter Gets Captured (Marvelettes)
https://www.youtube.com/watch?v=DBa746RVNHA
Bright Elusive Butterfly (Val Doonican)
https://www.youtube.com/watch?v=7FF0m-580B4
They're Coming to Take me (Napoleon XIV)
https://www.youtube.com/watch?v=BXOwNOf2QXY
There Goes My Everything (Humperdinck)
https://www.youtube.com/watch?v=ZtA_POLoXg4
I can Hear the Grass Grow (The Move)
https://www.youtube.com/watch?v=nDubIDZA9Jo

Knock on Wood (Eddie Floyd)
https://www.youtube.com/watch?v=Kceiks__PsE
I get around (The Beach Boys)
https://www.youtube.com/watch?v=wREBD2og5iY
Barbara Ann (The Beach Boys)
https://www.youtube.com/watch?v=vPRonG87eKw
California Girls (The Beach Boys)
https://www.youtube.com/watch?v=fmIsdMWzdaE
I love my Dog (Cat Stevens)
https://www.youtube.com/watch?v=xRWsh85P2T4
Matthew and Son (Cat Stevens)
https://www.youtube.com/watch?v=xRWsh85P2T4
Foxy Lady (Jimi Hendrix Experience)
https://www.youtube.com/watch?v=iy6WItWRKsQ
Fire (Jimi Hendrix Experience)
https://www.youtube.com/watch?v=cBGxX18O7CQ
Hey Joe (Jimi Hendrix Experience)
https://www.youtube.com/watch?v=rXwMrBb2x1Q
Purple Haze (Jimi Hendrix Experience)
https://www.youtube.com/watch?v=fjwWjx7Cw8I
Paper Sun (Traffic)
https://www.youtube.com/watch?v=bEnAft8bpBA
Something Stupid (Frank/Nancy Sinatra)
https://www.youtube.com/watch?v=pOiTv4MqK8M
Ten guitars (Englebert Humperdinck)
https://www.youtube.com/watch?v=4fxA7zLLQzY
Please Release Me (Englebert Humperdinck)
https://www.youtube.com/watch?v=kOcW9gZv68A
Make the world go away (Eddie Arnold)
https://www.youtube.com/watch?v=OAohfxCBDFE
Green Green Grass of Home (Tom Jones)
https://www.youtube.com/watch?v=4_3ghEaGt9s
Awkward Streak: Year of the Hamster.by Martin Wilkes

Awkward Streak is the charming story of a seven-year-old ruffian, growing up in the poverty-stricken suburbs of northern England, in 1963. Familiar smells, such as creosote, leather and treacle toffee, trigger the childhood memories of Martin Wells, whisking him back to a time when his 'awkward streak' dominated his life. Plagued by teachers, bullies, perverts, and even love, young Martin and his gang of ragamuffins, the 999ers, blunder through a series of shocking and often hilarious adventures. Martin shares his secrets with an unusual confidante, a hamster named Whiskey.

In this delightful tale, the author brilliantly captures the emerging sixties, from Babycham to The Beatles, through the lens of a child. Family dysfunction is slowly exposed, as he battles against his greatest enemy, which his parents call his 'awkward streak.' This heart-rending story will take you on an emotional roller-coaster, as you follow the exploits of the 999ers through the seasons, from the coldest winter, through the summer holidays and autumn, at a time when bonfire night was the biggest event of the year.

Awkward Streak is a classic, in the mould of *Adrian Mole* and *The Curious Incident of the Dog in the Night-time.*

https://www.amazon.co.uk/Awkward-Streak-Hamster-Martin-Wilkes-ebook/dp/B01CWO3152/ref=sr_1_2?s=books&ie=UTF8&qid=1499106985&sr=1-2&keywords=Awkward+Streak

269

Printed in Great Britain
by Amazon